To

Inkspell Holiday Delights

Fathers, Recipes, and Romance

Libby Kay, Liz Ashley, Laurel Houck,
Mark Love, Tammy Mannersly, Jennifer
Raines, Annie Grace Roberts, and
Isobel Reed

Inkspell Holiday Delights
Copyright © 2023 Inkspell Publishing
All rights reserved.

ISBN (ebook) 978-1-958136-74-4
(print) 978-1-958136-75-1

Inkspell Publishing
207 Moonglow Circle #101
Murrells Inlet, SC 29576

Cover art By Fantasia Frog Designs

PUBLISHER'S NOTE

Dad, Papa, Daddy, Grandpa, Poppi, Pa...Fathers, they go by many names and fill many roles. They are a daughter's first love, the person who teaches us about cars and sports. The guy who tells us to brush off that bloody knee or who pass on to us their love of golf. No matter if they are new fathers or have been a dad for a while. No matter if they are the fathers we were born to or the men who took on the important role, fathers hold a special place in our lives. And those special times are often intertwined with food. From that early morning breakfast, or the family recipe only they know how to make...The Inkspell Authors are sharing some of their favorite Fathers' stories and recipes with you!

Holidays are a special time filled with family, friends, and good food. As people gather, they talk about happy times, share stories, and pass on traditions to the younger generation. Not only do families share stories but authors also share stories. Ones that come from their dreams and heart.

We hope you will enjoy these delights...both of the food and book variety. And however you celebrate your holidays or gatherings, we hope you have many wonderful memories.

Thank you for purchasing this book and we hope you will go on to purchase some of the amazing books by these wonderful authors. They are available at various book sites in ebooks and print. You can find more about these books and author information at http://www.inkspellpublishing.com and on Facebook at https://www.facebook.com/InkspellPublishing.

DEDICATION

To the wonderful Inkspell Fathers and Father Figures who support us in so many ways...

To the enchanting readers who *always* share the love of their favorite books with others...

and to the amazing Inkspell authors who support each other like a family. <3

COMFORT FOR EVERY SEASON
By Libby Kay

In our family, food is important—like really important. And if you have read any of my Buckeye Falls books, you will see that with my characters. Food brings comfort no matter the situation or season, but it also brings people together.

Celebrating a milestone like a new job, engagement, or promotion? Get dolled up baby, because we're going out to dinner.

Mourning the loss of a love one? Get ready for an

avalanche of sandwich platters, casseroles, and baked goods. Fortunately, calories don't count during the grieving process. ♥

Having a great day? Why not go out and treat yourself?

Having a bad day? Why not go out and treat yourself? (You get the picture.) ☺

This anthology is to celebrate the father figures in our lives, and I'm fortunate enough to have a dad who instilled his love of food and family. We both share a sweet tooth, especially for cookies around the holidays and vanilla milkshakes any time of year. If only we both loved leafy greens as much, my cholesterol levels would be a lot happier.

My recipe and story follow our family's love of everyone's favorite comfort food—mac and cheese.

My earliest memories of eating mac and cheese are courtesy of my mom. This was one of our staple weeknight meals growing up, and I recall her making it after school. As the years went on, my dad started cooking outside the grill. He often took over mac and cheese duty, and the results were just as magically comforting.

There was a brief period in high school when everyone was busy with school and jobs, and I would volunteer to make mac and cheese so dinner would be ready when everyone came home. Maybe it was the freedom to cook on my own without interruptions, but I began to love spending time in the kitchen alone. Don't get me wrong, cooking with family are some of my favorite memories. But there is something to be said for blasting your favorite tunes while pottering around the kitchen getting your hands dirty. Plus, it was the late 90s, so the tunes were really good. (*NSYNC, if you're reading this I hope there's a reunion tour in 2024.)

My sister shares a deep love for this comfort classic, although our opinions differ on what to add to it. My sister is a purist, wanting only the divine combination of noodles and cheese. The older I get, the more I like to experiment and expand on the classic. Kathleen, when you read this, don't hate me for the mustard and Worcestershire sauce. I literally could not help myself. 😊

So, after years of eating—and loving—mac and cheese, my dad made this recipe at the exact perfect moment.

It was Christmas Eve about a decade ago. My husband and I had just moved over 13 hours away for work, and it was our first holiday back home. As soon as we stumbled inside, weighed down with luggage and presents and sore joints from way too long in a car, the aroma of melted cheese hit me square in the face. My knees went weak at the smell, and I could have cried tears of joy. This was the smell of my childhood, and I didn't realize how much I had missed it.

Dad walked out to greet us, a warm smile on his face. We made it just in time to eat before church (the Christmas Eve service is very important in our family), and dinner was ready. At this time, it was just five of us, and we sat around the table and devoured that mac and cheese like it was our last meal on earth. While sharing this gooey dream dinner, we caught up on life, work, and our plans after the winter holidays.

It was one of those perfect moments that I still look back on fondly. Everyone I loved in one room, sharing a meal and creating new memories. What could be more perfect? During trying and complicated times, I think back on moments like this and smile; knowing the world can be a safe place.

I don't know if my dad sensed how much I missed home after moving away, or if it was just dumb luck, but that was one of my favorite mac and cheese moments. I think that's the power of parents as we grow and have our own families. No matter what you're going through, you're still their child who needs a hug in more ways than one.

Fast forward and mac and cheese is still on the menu. I've shared this recipe with some of my in-laws, friends, and neighbors. It's my staple item to bring to potlucks, and don't get me started on how comforting it is during a certain time of the month. If I were a scientist, I'd run experiments on how noodles and cheese can make so many people happy. But that's not how my brain works, so instead I'll just eat and savor.

Whether or not you have a father, or father figure, in your life, I hope you will give this recipe a try. It is so versatile, you can add fancy cheeses, vegetables (roasted broccoli is a favorite of mine), or protein (did someone say bacon!?). Not only does it feel like a big hug, it's guaranteed to get a lot of smiles around the dinner table.

Happy eating everyone!

Recipe: Mac & Cheese

This can be a full meal or a side dish at the holidays. In my family, we serve with stewed tomatoes and baked beans to make a meal.

Ingredients:

- 1 pound of short cut pasta (like elbow or farfalle)
- 4 TB Butter
- 4 TB All-purpose flour
- 2-3 cups of milk (depending on how thick you like the sauce)
- 4 cups of cheese – I like a blend of 2 cheeses like sharp Cheddar, Swiss, or Havarti
- ½ cup grated parmesan mixed with 1 teas. paprika (for the topping)
- 2 teas. Dijon mustard
- 2 teas. Worcestershire sauce (optional)
- Salt and Pepper to taste

Instructions:

- Prep work:
  - Pre-heat oven to 350 degrees.
  - Lightly grease a 9x13" casserole dish.
  - Fill a stock pot with water and salt, bring to a boil.
  - In a small dish, mix parmesan with paprika.
  - Grate your cheeses. (Or buy pre-shredded and save yourself time.)

- Pasta:
    - When water is boiling, add pasta. Cook according to package instructions and drain. When dry, pour into prepared casserole dish.
    - I usually undercook by one minute since the noodles will continue cooking in the oven.

- Cheese Sauce:
    - In a small saucepan, melt butter. When melted and slightly foamy, add the flour and whisk until blended and smooth.
    - Let it cook for at least two minutes to cook off that raw flour taste.
    - Next, slowly pour in the milk while whisking. (A tip to avoid lumps → microwave your milk for one milk to take off the chill.)
    - When the milk is added, continue to stir until smooth.
    - Add the mustard, salt, pepper, and Worcestershire sauce.
    - Add cheeses and continue to stir until combined.
    - Remove from heat and add to casserole dish – stir until the pasta and sauce and all cozy. ☺
    - Top with the parmesan and paprika.
    - Bake uncovered for 30 minutes, or until it is bubbly and brown.
    - Enjoy with your favorite people!

SMALL TOWN, BUCKEYE FALLS, ROMANCES
by Libby Kay

FALLING HOME

Welcome to Buckeye Falls, Ohio!
'Tis the Season for Second Chances...And this couple is going to need a Christmas Miracle!

When New York transplant Ginny Meyer returns to her small hometown to help her father recover from surgery, she isn't looking for any complications. No Christmas caroling, no cookie decorating, and certainly no time spent with her ex-husband, Max. The trouble is, she's looped into helping with the Christmas Jubilee—and a certain ex is her planning partner. Now all her plans to avoid Max disappear in a puff of tinsel. But she can resist his charms, right?

Max Sanchez has three great loves in his life—his diner, Christmas, and his ex-wife. He's spent two years missing the woman who broke his heart and left town, and he'll use any excuse to spend time with her. Max hopes

some holiday cheer, and his famous cheese enchiladas, can help them find their way back together. Buckeye Falls hasn't felt the same since Ginny left, and Max can tell she's warming to the idea of staying in town. Now if only he could get her to stay with him…

With a little help from the residents of Buckeye Falls, this Christmas is bringing more than presents under the tree.

Author Libby Kay's books are perfect for fans of Kristan Higgins' second chance romances or Sharon Sala's smalltown romances. Readers will fall in love with Buckeye Falls, Ohio and the townspeople as they embrace the holiday season. Slip in to this enchanting smalltown and stay awhile! You might just fall in love…

EXCERPT:

Blinking, Ginny begged her eyes to see someone else standing before her. It was as if her memories willed themselves back to life. Beside her, her father perked up and lifted his free hand. "Max, over here." Max turned around, and Ginny felt the air leave her lungs. This was no trick of her mind. It was the real deal. *Well, hell …*

Time had been good to Max; there was no denying it. His dark hair was longer now, curling at the base of his neck. A few flecks of gray threatened to take over his temples, but he managed to look mature rather than haggard. Instead of the clean-shaven face she remembered, his chiseled jawline was now peppered with a few days of stubble. Suddenly, Ginny understood all the fuss with lumbersexuals.

Max's brown eyes darkened when he saw her, but his steps didn't falter. "Harold, good to see you." He moved one of his shopping bags to his other arm and shook her father's hand. When he turned to her, Ginny felt her breath hitch as he reached out his hand for a shake. *Really? They were in the hand-shaking phase of their relationship?*

Ginny reached out and took his hand, a shot of

awareness coursing through her body as his fingers wrapped around hers. "Max," she said his name in greeting, hoping her tone was light, carefree.

"Gin." Max swallowed and squeezed her hand before letting it go. He didn't say anything at first, just studied her. She was glad she had listened to her father about makeup. Bumping into her ex-husband with bedhead and sans mascara would have been mortifying.

Ginny was helpless for a moment, staring at Max like a fool. Perhaps she'd fallen into an alternate universe when she left the turnpike? Maybe her rental car was a time machine where she felt pulled to a man who bruised her heart? A man whose heart was certainly broken by her.

Either oblivious or uncaring of her current slack-jawed state, Max surprised her by stepping closer and giving her a genuine smile. "I'm glad you're back," he said. "It's really good to see you."

In that moment, staring into his warm gaze, Ginny couldn't disagree. Being so close to Max, so close to the worn paths of their past, she felt comfortable. This didn't feel like a foreign place; it felt like home.

FALLING FOR YOU

Welcome to Buckeye Falls, Ohio!
Sparks fly in this small town as everyone's favorite gruff pastry chef finally gives the sweetest guy in town a chance.

CeCe LaRue knows what she wants in life, and in the kitchen, and that's control. She doesn't have time for distractions—from her past or present. But that doesn't mean a certain bright-eyed coworker hasn't captured her heart.

Evan Lawson is a chronic optimist, and he brings his sunny disposition to everything he does, especially his job at the diner. It's obvious why he loves his job so much, and it has everything to do with CeCe. He's been crushing on her for a while, but he's biding his time. Much like the perfect recipe, love cannot be rushed.

When a major food competition comes to town, Evan is thrilled at the prospect of competing. Despite her stellar culinary skills, CeCe is hesitant to participate. The celebrity chef host is more than a pretty face; he's the painful past she's been outrunning for years.

Can CeCe open herself up to the prospect of love and give Evan a chance? Can Evan's optimism keep them both afloat?

Falling For You is part of the Buckeye Falls series and can be enjoyed as a stand-alone read. Author Libby Kay's books are perfect for fans of Penny Reid and Sharon Sala's smalltown romances. These sweet romances will have readers falling in love with Buckeye Falls, Ohio. Slip in to this enchanting smalltown and stay awhile! You might just fall in love…

EXCERPT:
They were friends, friends with a whole lot of potential. Surely this magnetic pull wasn't one-sided?

"I think I could be serious about you," CeCe finally said, the words shaking Evan back to the moment. "And I don't know what to do about that."

Evan felt his heart explode in his chest. "You do?"

CeCe slowly raised her hand and cupped his cheek, having to stand on tiptoe to make up for their height difference. How easily he forgot her height when they were together. She was such a force, she filled up every space she was in. Her energy, her passion for what she did, radiated around her.

Even now, standing outside with only the din of the pub surrounding them, CeCe was all he could see, feel, and touch. Her thumb swiped around his lips, making him shiver. "I do."

Words escaping him, Evan closed the distance to kiss her. It was slow, tender. They were feeling each other out, finding the angles where they fit best. Cradling her face in his hands, the world around them evaporated. CeCe moaned, and Evan swallowed it, wanting to savor every little thing she gave him. Kissing CeCe felt crucial, like he'd die without her touch, die without having the privilege of her.

FALLING AGAIN

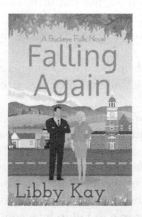

Welcome back to Buckeye Falls, Ohio!
Does this small town mayor have the political

savvy to negotiate his way back into his wife's heart?

From the outside, Mayor Anthony Snyder and his wife Natalie have it all. Adorable children, a lovely home, and a never-ending supply of free food from the local diner. But behind closed doors, this duo struggles to stay connected. The sparkle they show Buckeye Falls has turned a little dull on the home front.

Over the last decade, things became hectic in the Snyder household. Anthony was elected to office, following in his father's footsteps. Unfortunately, he's reminded regularly that these are big shoes to fill. Being the best mayor takes a lot of time—time he's not spending with his family.

Natalie prides herself on being everything to everyone, but the job of a wife hasn't been smooth sailing. Wrapped up in her own growing business and their kids' activities, her time with Anthony has dwindled faster than her secret stash of Halloween candy. Natalie longs for quality time with the man she loves, but it never seems to be in the cards.

A chance to visit their family lake house promises a week away from it all, but can these two reconnect when there's no distractions? Or is it time for these high achievers to admit that love might be the one thing they can't master?

With a little help from the residents of Buckeye Falls, this power couple will find their way back to happily ever after.

Falling Again is the third book in the Buckeye Falls series, but it can be enjoyed as a standalone read. Featuring similar marriage conflicts as in Lyssa Kay Adams' The Bromance Book Club and the small-town romance of Susan Mallery's Fool's Gold series, fans will love this second chance love story. After all, who doesn't deserve to fall in love again?

EXCERPT:

"Anthony saw me topless, and vice versa, for the first time in ages yesterday."

Ginny raised an eyebrow. "Isn't that a good thing?"

"It would be if we'd done anything about it. Both times we were cleaning up after the kids and didn't even acknowledge it happened. Or I guess that it didn't happen."

Ginny paused, clearly unsure how to continue. "Has it been a while since you two—" she swirled her mug in the air, gesturing for Natalie to finish the sentence. Apparently, her friend wasn't going easy on her this morning.

"Had sex? Yes. It's been a while. It's been so long that I don't even remember the basic mechanics of the deed. And don't even ask me when it was. Sometime between Otis's conception and last Thursday." Natalie sank back in her chair and groaned. "This is bad."

*

Placing her hand over his mouth to shut him up, Natalie shook her head. "Stop that. You are a wonderful husband and father. Just because we hit a rough patch doesn't mean all the ways you love us don't shine through." Beneath her hand, Anthony sighed. He sounded so defeated; she wanted to wrap him in a blanket and hide him from the world. "I've made some mistakes too. You're not allowed to play the blame game alone. It's a two-player game." Lowering her hand, she saw a little smirk cross Anthony's face before he sighed again.

"You're letting me off too easily, Nat."

"I don't think so. I'm trying to give you some grace. I think we both deserve a little of that, don't you?"

FAKING THE FALL

Sparks fly when a reclusive artist meets his muse in this new installment of the Buckeye Falls series.

Alice Snyder knows her reputation—and if she didn't, Buckeye Falls loves to remind her. She may come from the town's First Family, but that doesn't mean she plays by the rules. After a decade of traveling and going to school, she's back home and ready to settle down, or at least relax for a while. The trouble is, her neighbors are determined to find her a husband. She needs a way to get them off her back…

When James Gibson, a divorced artist, flees New York for the peace of small-town Ohio, he's excited to get painting again. The only trouble is, he's completely blocked. Despite his best efforts, his collection of canvases are blank and he's at a career crossroads. A chance meeting with the mayor's sister throws James's routine off balance, and he's eager to spend more time with this quirky spitfire.

And Alice might have the solution to both their problems…

Fake Date.

She gets the Nosey Nellies off her back, and James gets time with a woman who inspires him both inside and outside the studio.

Just a few weeks of pretending, and they'll move on. Simple, right? The trouble is the more time they spend together, the realer their relationship feels. The laughter, the stolen kisses—it all starts to feel like more.

Can these two be honest with each other and find their happily-ever-after, or are they doomed for a real breakup?

Libby Kay's FAKING THE FALL redeems Buckeye Falls's spinster troublemaker with a fake relationship romance filled with sweet small town vibes. FAKING THE FALL will bring to mind amazing books like Practice Makes Perfect by Sarah Adams and Fix Her Up by Tessa Bailey. But best of all, it returns readers to the small Ohio town and the familiar characters from the previous Buckeye Falls books. All the zany, overbearing, and well-meaning ones! So sit back and grab FAKING THE FALL for the latest roller-coaster romance by Libby Kay.

EXCERPTS:
Alice's early thoughts on James
James agreed to her fake dating plan. Alice would be lying if she wasn't already excited to see him again. Her skin still burned—yes, burned—from where he'd touched her. For all the men she claimed to love before, none of them elicited that reaction with a simple touch.

James Gibson was fire—plain and simple.

James's early thoughts on Alice
There was this urge to keep Alice protected, to ensure she was safe. And it certainly didn't feel remotely fake to him. This felt like the beginning of something big—something real. James's mind was on fire with thoughts of Alice, of the art he wanted to create. His heart hadn't pounded like this since his divorce, and he had hope that he was on his way back to himself. Buckeye Falls turned out to be better for him than he had expected. And then there was Alice. His world had been so gray and lifeless this last year. But Alice promised an abundance of color.

ABOUT THE AUTHOR

Libby Kay lives in the city in the heart of the Midwest with her husband. When she's not writing, Libby loves reading romance novels of any kind. Stories of people falling in love nourish her soul. Contemporary or Regency, sweet or hot, as long as there is a happily ever after she's in love!

When not surrounded by books, Libby can be found baking in her kitchen, binging true crime shows, or on the road with her husband, traveling as far as their bank account will allow.

Writing is a solitary job, and Libby loves to hear from readers. Reach out and review her stories anytime. She'd love to hear from you.

Website: https://www.libbykayauthor.com/

Facebook: @LibbyKayAuthor

Goodreads: Libby Kay

Instagram: https://www.instagram.com/libbykayauthor/

Bookbub: https://www.bookbub.com/profile/libby-kay

A GRAND HEART
By Liz Ashlee

There aren't grand stories to tell about my dad, but instead vignettes. Fitting because while my dad has a grand heart, he isn't the person who is going to go out of his way to be seen. He likes to be in the background, with his intelligence, helpfulness, and care are always available to be offered.

Kentucky sees snowfall every year, some years more than others; unfortunately, most are only a disappointing few inches. But one of my happiest memories of my dad is when it would snow and we would both get bundled up, with Mom promising hot chocolate later. Dad's job was to shovel the driveway, mine was to relish in the layer of snow while it lasted. We had a great hill for sledding—it sloped down into a cul-de-sac—but for some reason, I wanted Dad to pull me around in my bright pink sled instead. So, he did—he pulled me up the hill, down the hall, sideways. As an adult, my first thought is, *My God, didn't his back hurt?* But he fought through it—or maybe the cold was numbing the pain!—to make me happy.

When I was in sixth grade, one of my biggest dreams came true—Dad took me to work for "Take your Child to Work Day." I remember the skirt and shirt I wore so I would look my most professional—as if I could hide the fact that I was a twelve-year-old girl. After meeting his co-workers and seeing his building, we took our seats in his cubicle. Little did I know how boring adult jobs are. Dad gave me a notebook to keep me occupied. I drew and wrote stories in it, and didn't think anything about it. But when Dad switched jobs, he brought home the notebook. He'd kept it in his desk drawer all those years because the pages held something I'd created.

Toward the end of high school, I was the field commander for my high school marching band. During my senior year, our show was themed around the Beatles. I wore a dress with the Union Jack on it and a pair of white gogo boots. Honestly, I never felt cooler...except the downside was that I had to climb up onto my podium in gogo boots in front of bleachers full of people and a field full of my friends. Because my dad was a "band dad" he always helped the pit or set up the props, but above all else, he was the hand that helped guide me up onto that podium. He saved me from what could have been the most mortifying fall of my teenage life.

In college, when I finally got the courage to send a book around to publishers *and* was accepted by Inkspell, my dad was the first one to purchase my book. He always is. And throughout the process of writing, editing, cover-design, he always asks for updates. His favorite question being, "When can I order it?" As soon as I give him the go-ahead, he buys it in print and ebook to show his support.

When I was dating my now-husband, Nathan, one of my best-loved moments with my dad happened—it's our favorite to reflect on, honestly. I had just gotten a new TV and Dad was going to wall-mount it in my bedroom at their house. Nathan came over to help. My dad promptly gave him the tools and instructions, then made him do it, watching him every step of the way. My dad likes to make people do things on their own so he can teach them. But why wouldn't he have made me do it, then? We think it was a test to make sure Nathan was worthy of me—a test Nathan obviously passed. I love that memory in particular because it was the start of their relationship. My dad gained a son in Nathan—someone he can do projects with, like carving doors out of slabs or renovating a bathroom.

All of these moments are my dad supporting me, encouraging me and lifting me up (sometimes literally). They're examples of his love not always spoken, but *always* felt. My dad is the man who loved me first and will love me always, and that makes me the luckiest daughter.

ROB'S CLASSIC BURGER

Ingredients

1. 1 lb beef
2. Buns

Instructions

1. Create beef patties, then cook on medium until preferred doneness. (If you're Rob, then that's so done, even a Ouija board can't communicate with the cow)
2. Place patties on buns, without cheese, pickles, onions, ketchup, etc.
3. Serve with tater tots on the side (also eaten without any condiments).

CONTEMPORARY ROMANCES
By Liz Ashlee

STEP TOWARD YOU

Step One: We admitted we were powerless over alcohol-that our lives had become unmanageable.

There are twelve steps in Alcoholics Anonymous and Silas Manning knows all of them by heart. He's been living them since a drunk driving accident resulted in the destruction of three lives. When he meets Rooney Oliver, he quickly realizes you can be addicted to things other than alcohol—you can be addicted to people, too.

Rooney's mother is dying and Rooney feels like she's dying with her. It's not until Silas comes into their lives that any of them start feeling hope—but Silas isn't ready to let go of the past or open himself up to a future.

Sometimes the only person who you want to lose is yourself.

EXCERPT:

"Step Ten. Continued to take personal inventory and when we were wrong, promptly admitted it," Silas answers after a long gap of silence. His fingers curl around the Tupperware containers he's holding. His jaw clenches, and his eyes flash with an intensity different from anything else I've seen from him.

Sure, before, I could tell he was checking me out, and there was an intensity in his eyes which was blatant lust, but this intensity I can't describe. It's almost like he's grasping desperately at something he can't seem to reach. I wish he could. I think he needs it.

"I wronged you, Rooney."

His saying my name makes my heart trip. His voice isn't allowed to have that power. I need to hate him for the way he treated me, so I can my protect myself. I don't need any more damage than I've already taken. The armor around my heart is about as thin the plastic wrap on these muffins.

I don't know what else to do but follow him. I sift his words over in my head. The only way he's wronged me is by being so heartless, but it feels like there's more to it than that, as if I'm not the only one he's trying to apologize to. For someone who works so hard to stay distant, maybe he's the opposite of distant, which is why he's trying so badly to hide away.

SORT OF NORMAL

Falling in love isn't as easy as staying in love.

Carter Hart and Boone Fell's lives are tangle of perfect and imperfect memories. In a world of drugs, alcoholism and neglectful parents, their love for each other kept them strong. But all it takes is one kiss and a lie to tear them apart.

When Carter's brother, Declan, dies of an overdose, Boone decides he can't let another day of secrets and mistaken circumstances keep them apart. His only problem? Now that he's ready to move forward with Carter, she's ready to leave him where she thinks he belongs: in the past.

EXCERPT:

"None of this is what I wanted to talk about," Boone says, sounding frustrated, as we come to a halt at the intersection for my street.

"What did you want to talk about?"

"You." He takes a step into my space and looks down at me. He brings his hands up as if he were going to touch me, but then he doesn't. If there's one thing overly-flirtatious, charming, talkative Boone is good at, it's putting up barriers. He's the king of keeping you at a distance, even when he's right in front of you. He manages to do it in a way that makes you look as though you were the one putting them up. "I miss you, Carter. So goddamn much. Not having you in my life is hell. I meant it when I said I miss you."

"Boone," I say softly. "I'm not sure I can do this with you."

"I know I don't deserve it."

"It's not that."

"Well, it sort of is."

I can't hold back a smile. He's just so blunt. "It's just, I can't go through losing someone again," I continue.

"What if you don't lose me this time?"

"I think that every time, and I somehow still do."

"This time is going to be different. I'm going to prove I'm not leaving again." "It's not really something you can prove." I bite my tongue as I carefully construct my words. "There's always someday. *Today* you might not leave, but *someday* you could. I haven't been able to trust in the *always* sense."

"Let me give you that, then."

"I don't know if you can."

"I can, and I will."

HEART'S A MESS

Sometimes our hearts break…

When John Smith's father was dying, his family knew there was nothing to do, but they tried anyway. Paying more money than they had, they took John's father and the last of their hope to Ezra Abel for a healing.

And we fight to keep it beating…

But Ezra's faith healing is only a trick—a way to fool families out of their money. Worst of all, he humiliates these families when they're at their lowest. After his father dies, John devotes his life to revealing Ezra for the evil person he is. And when Kinley walks into his life, he's much closer to accomplishing his goal.

But all you can do is hold it in your hands.

Kinley Abel is Ezra's weapon, milking families of their hard-earned cash. She doesn't want to do her father's bidding, but she has to. Except the more she falls for John, the more she questions her role in the church, leading her down a dangerous path which could break her heart.

Sometimes you fall in love with lies.

EXCERPT:

Bea's voice removes me from the past. Thank God I

haven't had to witness something as what happened to my dad again.

"Thank you, Ezra," she says, then kneels—throwing a grin toward the crowd—to kiss his hand. No one notices she isn't thanking the big guy upstairs.

Ezra pats her head as if she were a child and says something to her that no one else can hear, before stepping around her and holding his arms up similar to a ring leader in the grand finale. Behind him, Bea exits back off the stage. She is walking perfectly straight, although slower than I'd imagine someone who is "healed" might walk. Instead, it's as if her mind is telling her something that her body isn't.

I don't think false confidence or mind over matter are entries in the bible, although Ezra brandishes them like weapons.

When Ezra faces us all, he's toting a deadly sin—pride. Maybe he believes he did heal her—not God. *Him.*

"The Lord Jesus will always answer our call so long as we hold our faith in God. As long as I lead this church, God will be in our audience. I promise you all that He will heal and help those who have opened their heart to our church."

And their wallets.

WISHING ON WATER

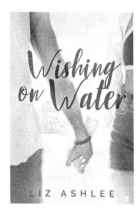

People getting engaged. Married. Adopting pets. Buying cars and houses. Having babies. Meanwhile, Hope is still living with her parents, hasn't accomplished anything since high school and her relationship status isn't just single – it's non-existent.

As she sees it, there's nothing else to do but the one thing that makes the most logical sense: flee to her great-aunt's retirement community. The last thing she expects is to meet a very handsome, very *age appropriate* man there who might be the key to solving her single relationship problem.

EXCERPT:

"Lucky us," Aunt Isla says, crinkling her nose. Someone knocks on the door and she stares at it blankly. "Who's that?"

Arthur's smile melts away. "Paul. My competition."

Aunt Isla laughs. "With all the excitement over Hope, I completely forgot I asked Paul to stop by to look at my TV." She claps her hands together excitedly. If I didn't know any better, I'd almost think there's a conspiratorial tint to her eyes. "Oh, I can't wait for you to meet Paul,

Hope. He's such a sweetheart."

"And a dreamboat," I add.

"The man has more girlfriends around here than you can count and you'll see why," she says, walking toward the door. "Coming!"

I spin in my chair, resting my arms on the back of it. I don't know why I'm so excited to meet this Paul. He's a looking glass into what a gorgeous guy looks like in the eyes of a retiree. Evidently he's deaf, but a veteran, and he must be handy—but is he only attractive because he's handy? My mom used to say there's nothing more attractive than a man who is willing to work without issue. Then again, maybe he's like Harrison Ford and manages to stay young because of a certain rugged handsomeness and a lot of personality.

Only the door opens up and I'm wrong about it all.

About fifty years wrong.

"You're the dreamboat?" I blurt out.

MAGIC & MISCHIEF

Whether Gods or Demons, when romance and magic mix, anything is possible. Join Inkspell authors as they enchant you with these NINE stories filled with supernatural twists and turns!

Everwood Academy by Clara Winter
With the casting of a single spell, Grace's world falls apart. Enrolled in Everwood Academy, the teen discovers that darkness is everywhere, leading her into a dangerous trap where even her new friends won't be able to save her.

Don't Mess with the Gods by Mark Love and Elle Nina Castle
Solana doubts her sanity when four Greek gods visit. Enter psychiatrist Dr. Michael Granger. Two people existing. Leave it to the Greek gods to help them live a little.

Vital Impetus by VK Tritschler
Lost between worlds, Jess is hunted. Fighting back using newfound powers the teen has yet to understand, her only help is an old childhood friend with secrets of his own. Will their reunion be her salvation or the end of her life?

Breath of Life by Kristy Centeno
In a blink of an eye, Arie Garcia is thrust into a dangerous world--unsure if the man claiming to be her savior is in fact one...or...something much worse.

My Soul to Save by Nicole Sobon
Some birthdays are special. Mine proves to be life altering. I only hope I can survive it.

The Urn in the Attic by Liz Ashlee
Anna, Dani and Wilson only want to clean out their attic, but they find an urn. When weird things happen around the house, is it an unwanted entity...or just the cat?

The Curse of Cinder Ash by Mikaël Lemieux

Plagued by a curse and ruled by evil, a traveler must save the town of Cinder Ash to find a piece of his soul.

Through the Mirror by Majanka Verstraete

As a Gatekeeper, sixteen-year-old Aster protects innocent people from demons, and sends them back through mirrors—gates—to hell. When Collin Mortimer, a Dark Caster and one of the most popular guys in school, asks Aster for help and she accepts, it might be the deadliest mistake of her life.

Curses, Quests and Cuties by Celia Mulder

A love story no one asked for set in motion by a curse no one can break.

ABOUT THE AUTHOR

Liz Ashlee is an avid romance reader and the author of *Step Toward You* and *Sort of Normal*. She recently earned her Master of Arts in English degree from Northern Kentucky, where she also earned her undergraduate degrees. Liz lives in Kentucky, where she loves spending time with her parents, fiancé, friends, dog, and cat.

Website: https://www.liz-ashlee.com/
Facebook: https://www.facebook.com/LizAshleeAuthor/
Instagram: https://www.instagram.com/lizashleeauthor/
Twitter: https://twitter.com/lizashleeauthor?lang=en

FATHERS & FOOD
By Laurel Houck

Dad taught me many things. Find humor and joy in any situation. Be yourself—I'll always love you no matter what. Faith is the only foundation.

He did *not* teach me about nutrition. This man ate *no* fruits or veggies. None. If served cottage cheese on a lettuce leaf in a restaurant, he wouldn't touch it. His idea of a salad bar was croutons, cheese, and hard-boiled egg. All one hundred forty-five pounds of him existed on meat, potatoes, pasta, and vanilla wafers from a box.

Once in a while he took a walk on the wild side. On a special occasion he would indulge in a small piece of Mom's pecan pie hidden under a mountain of whipped cream.

I continue to make the same recipe today. And with each sweet bite—liberally garnished with whipped cream of course—I remember the first guy who stole my heart. And who holds it still.

JUNE'S PECAN PIE

One unbaked 9 ½ " or two 8" unbaked pie crusts

5 eggs
1 cup white sugar
1 ½ cups corn syrup
½ teaspoon salt
1 ½ teaspoon real vanilla
1 ½ cups chopped pecans
6 tablespoons melted butter

Whipped cream

1. Beat eggs and sugar together.
2. Add corn syrup, salt, vanilla, chopped pecans, and butter.
3. Mix thoroughly.
4. Pour into unbaked pie shell.
5. Bake at 325 degrees until filling is set, about 1 ¼ hours.

Garnish with whipped cream.

PARANORMAL YOUNG ADULT LOVE STORIES
By Laurel Houck

THE GIRL WITH CHAMELEON EYES

It's an abrupt, uncomfortable incarnation for Summer, the ghostly girl with chameleon eyes. Exotic hues roil in her gaze as she seeks to recall what awful sin in her past has doomed her to roam the earth. And to discover what—or who—will bring her to eternal rest.

Kota, brunt of bad jokes because he's different, feels an instant connection to Summer. She recoils at the mere sight of him. Yet they are drawn together in a dance of mutual need, choreographed by the ages.

As Summer grows more attached to both her young foster brother and to Kota's friend, Preston, she struggles against complacency. Until discovering that if she doesn't expiate the guilt on her soul by her seventeenth birthday, she will roam forever.

For her, it's hate at first sight. For him, it's instant attraction. When the pieces of their lives begin to unravel and intertwine, will love be enough to save them both? Or will evil decide their future?

EXCERPT:

My vapor solidifies with no warning whatsoever. Abrupt. Compact. Unexpected.

I'm near a dumpster that squats behind a floodlit Sheetz gas station, the stench of hot dog grease and burnt coffee strong in my nostrils. My feet are last to materialize, so that for a moment when I look down, I'm floating about five inches above the pavement, white mist above black asphalt.

With the physical transformation comes the rest of it. Light and cool converts to heavy and hot. Yearning and searching morphs to fear and uncertainty. Naked and misty transforms to flesh-bound and clothed. I'm grateful for the garments that cover my skin, even if how that happens is a mystery to me.

The nausea and dizziness are stronger than the last time I can recall. I lean against the dumpster and slide to the ground, knees up, head in my hands. It will pass soon. I hope.

"Miss, are you okay?" A deep voice rumbles above the traffic noise. The tall, ruddy-faced cop is standing over me, wearing a black uniform and a hat with a band of navy and gold squares. "I'm Officer Sullivan. Did someone hurt you?"

"I'm fine." I scramble to my feet, glad it's dim in the shadow of the dumpster. I'm still shaky and have no clue what color has risen in my eyes. Between the lights and my startling arrival, anything is possible.

I keep my head down. What can I tell him? I know that I used to be alive, that now I'm a ghost, and that I'm searching for something to expiate my guilt over...what? Beyond that, fuzzy at best.

LOVE IS A RIVER

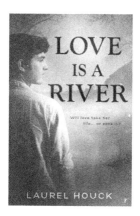

Love dies with Abby's father. The return of her mother after a twelve-year absence brings more grief. And the move to a dilapidated house along the Youghiogheny River bike trail is an exile.

When blond, blue-eyed Jack rides into Abby's life, it's like the sun has been restored to her world. Bit by bit, hints of a darker side to his personality appear. She struggles to deny them, even while her best friend, Morton, grows increasingly mistrustful of the handsome stranger.

Abby uncovers a mystery from the Civil War era in a nearby cemetery, which brings her only moments of peace. Cool caresses and the whispered call, "Abigail…" send her digging into the past.

But as Jack's motives become ever more unclear, the love Abby hoped for seems impossible. And leads her to a life or death choice. Will love be her salvation … or her demise?

EXCERPT:

A floorboard creaked over her head, and she stopped, her senses on high alert. Ghosts? Serial killer? She pressed her fingertips against the rough plaster wall, her ears tuned into every nuance of sound, her eyes scanning the stairwell. Stale air clogged her lungs, and the metallic taste of fear drenched her mouth. She had read about murdered girls in abandoned houses. Thick old walls didn't let screams—or people—escape.

A door squeaked, a slow, deliberate sound followed by a stealthy footstep.

Abby waited in the curve of the stairs, back pressed against the wall. Her thin black sweater clung to her suddenly damp skin, and the urge to pee made her squirm. Footsteps came closer. She sniffed a sudden whiff of chocolate. The hair on her arms stood straight up, threaded between the goose bumps raised there. Her heart labored harder, a painful drumbeat in her chest. A dust mote floated through the air, tickling her nose with the threat of a sneeze. She held her breath, fight or flight vying for her attention. But if she didn't handle this, Lisa might get hurt, too.

Taking a deep breath, she peered around the corner.

A piercing shriek split her eardrums. "Ahhhhh."

ABOUT THE AUTHOR

Laurel has been writing since the age of six, when Crawls the Caterpillar inched across her lined notebook paper propelled by a fat yellow pencil. She has published magazine and newspaper articles as well as blog posts with AllthewayYA, seapc.org, and on her website. Her portfolio includes multiple children's stories from picture books, to Middle Grade, to Young Adult. The Girl With Chameleon Eyes debuted with Inkspell Publishing in March of 2018.

In addition to writing, her passion is for travel to exotic locations around the globe. The people she meets, the places she visits, and the quirky way she looks at life all inspire her work. She loves complex characters and intricate plots that mesh into multifaceted books, melding romance, mystery, adventure, and history.

Laurel was a chosen participant at Better Books, a craft-based workshop near San Francisco. She is active in the Society of Children's Book Writers and Illustrators, and has been a presenter at their Fall SCBWI Conference

In Pittsburgh.

When she's not deep into a writing project, Laurel is a medical missions' nurse, traveling for Southeast Asia Prayer Center, Hope in Haiti, Caring Hearts, and Convoy of Hope. She lives in Pittsburgh, Pennsylvania, with her husband and their fur baby, Mable. All of that, plus she's the world's biggest fan of chocolate milkshakes and hugs.

Website: www.laurelhouckpages.com
Facebook: Laurel Houck
Twitter: @LaurelHouck
Instagram: laurelscottage

FATHER'S TALE
By Mark Love

I'm a lucky guy.

I'm the proud father of two amazing sons. Being a part of their lives, offering a little support and guidance along the way will always be one of my greatest accomplishments. The memories of some of their escapades as they were growing still bring a smile to my face.

Here's a favorite.

Cameron, my younger son, was starting middle school. That's seventh and eighth grade in this area. At the end of the first week of classes in September, the school hosted 'Activity Night'. This would include access to the gym, game stations in the halls and a DJ playing music. Cameron had been looking forward to this for weeks and was anxious for the fun to start.

"I'm going inside to see if they need any volunteers to help chaperone." I'd assisted with similar events when Travis, my older son, was in middle school.

"I'll meet you at the flagpole afterwards."

"Cool," Cameron said. With that, he disappeared into the crowd of kids.

Turns out they did need my help. I was given the details for four different stations. The plan was to move to each new spot every half hour. The two hours would pass quickly.

During the evening, I saw many kids from Cameron's elementary school. They would wave or say hello. Cameron and a few of his buddies would zoom by periodically, all flashing big smiles.

At the end of the evening, I met him at the flagpole. Back in the car, I asked if he had a good time.

"I had a <u>great</u> time. And I made ten bucks!"

Now I was confused. "How did you make ten bucks?"

"Some of the girls paid me to dance with them."

I had to bite my lip to keep from laughing. "There's a term for that: gigolo."

"Really?"

"It's not something to aspire to. Why would girls pay you to dance?"

Cameron shrugged. "It wasn't my idea. One girl said nobody would dance with her. Then she offered me a dollar, so I danced with her. Then another girl gave me a dollar. It kept going from there. Promise you won't tell Mom."

All I could do was shake my head. "I'm not telling her. You are."

"No way! She'll get mad and make me pay them back."

"Think about this. All the girls that paid you, their mothers know your mom. Once those girls talk with their mothers, your mom is liable to get calls. It's better that you tell her up front."

Reluctantly, he agreed. When we got home, he fessed up. My wife, in her wisdom, let him keep the money, but he had to promise to dance with each of those girls at the next 'Activity Night'. And he couldn't charge them!

CHICKEN PICCATTA

I've been making this dish for years and it's always a hit. This goes well with pasta, tossed salad, a crusty loaf of bread, and wine. (Some people will substitute apple juice for the wine)

Prep time to table: 30 minutes

2 boneless, skinless chicken breasts
6-8 ounces of fresh mushrooms
¼ cup of flour
¼ cup of white wine (Reisling is good)
Half of a lemon
3 tablespoons of oil or butter.
1 teaspoon of capers

Preheat a large skillet at medium high for 7 minutes.

If the breasts are thick, slice them horizontally first. Some cooks prefer to place them between sheets of waxed paper and flatten them with a mallet, but cutting is easier. Then slice the chicken into thin strips. Dredge the chicken lightly in the flour and set aside.

Clean and slice the mushrooms, then set aside.

Slice the lemon in half. Using a small knife, cut into each section to loosen any seeds. You can use a lemon press to catch the seeds or pick them out before adding the juice.

When the skillet is ready, add the oil or butter. As the oil sizzles, slowly add the chicken. Let it cook for 3 to 4 minutes before turning. The chicken should be golden brown. Cook another 3 minutes, then add the mushrooms, the lemon juice and the white wine. Mix well, to get the mushrooms down into the heat. Stir occasionally. Cook for another 3 minutes. Remove from heat.

Garnish with capers.

Enjoy!

THE JAMIE RICHMOND MYSTERIES
By Mark Love

DEVIOUS

Jamie Richmond, reporter turned author, is doing research for her next book. Attempting to capture the realism of a police officer's duties while on patrol, she manages to tag along for a shift with a state police trooper. A few traffic stops and a high speed chase later, Jamie's ride takes an unexpected turn when she witnesses the trooper being shot.

Although it is not a fatal injury, Jamie becomes obsessed with unraveling the facts behind this violent act. While she is trying to sort out this puzzle, she becomes romantically involved with Malone, another trooper with a few mysteries of his own. Now Jamie's attention is divided between a blooming romance and solving the crime which is haunting her.

Jamie begins to question the events that took place and exactly who could be behind the shooting. It was a devious mind. But who?

EXCERPT:

Suddenly, I saw a flash of light and heard a muffled bang. Smitty pitched onto his back, his right hand clawing feebly at his holster as a loud roar reached my ears. The door of the truck was still open, a brown arm extended beyond the edge of the spotlight. A gun was clutched in the gloved hand. I watched in horror as the trigger was pulled back for another shot.

Everything that happened next must have been instinct. Or maybe it was merely a reaction. Or dumb luck. Or the Force. Yeah, maybe it was the Force. I don't think I'll ever know for sure.

I reached across and pounded on the horn with one hand, flipping the buttons Smitty had used to activate the siren with the other. The sudden noise startled the driver. His arm jerked back into the cab and the door slammed. Spraying stones and dust behind, the truck lurched onto the road and raced away.

Fumbling the microphone off the dash, I thumbed the button. "Kleinschmidt has been shot! Send an ambulance!" I dropped the microphone and managed to get my door open. The frame around the window clipped my forehead and knocked me back a step.

I'd forgotten to turn off the siren and its wail was splitting my eardrums. "Idiot," I muttered, "stay calm." This was easier to say than it ever was to do.

Reaching back inside, I switched the siren off then rushed around to the front of the car. Smitty was lying on his back on the edge of the road. Blood soaked the gravel beneath him. His eyes were closed, but I could see his chest moving.

I dropped to my knees beside him. "You're going to be okay, Smitty. I called for help."

VANISHING ACT

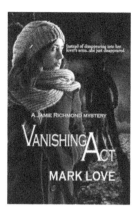

When Jamie's best friend vanishes, she'll do anything to find her and bring her home.

A new year marks new beginnings for Jamie Richmond. Not only has she moved into a cozy new house, but she's brought Malone along with her to fan the flames of their growing romance. When Jamie's best friend, Linda Davis, enters the picture, she thinks everything is right with the world.

Linda begins a May-September romance with Vincent Schulte, Jamie's doctor and good friend. But while Vince is sweeping Linda off her feet, she unknowingly has captured the attention of a stalker. The idyllic life suddenly takes a very bad turn when Linda disappears without a trace on a cold and snowy day. The police are scrambling to find a clue that will lead them to Linda.

Malone does his best to comfort Jamie and encourages her to let the professionals do their job. But if there's one thing he's learned in their time together, it's that nothing will stop this stubborn redhead from solving this mystery.

Jamie turns all of her attention on figuring out who took Linda and where she might be, regardless of the dangers she may face. Her efforts once again put her in harm's way. But will she find her best friend?

EXCERPT:

"So are you going to tell me what's going on, Linda? You've been beaming a thousand-watt smile."

I saw the color radiate on her cheeks. She lowered her eyes and took a sip of her coffee. Finally, she drew a deep breath and raised her face.

"I think I'm in love."

I sat back in amazement.

"Vince came over last night. After dinner, we moved to the sofa. The fire was lit and one light was on low. I had been in a rush when I came home, so I hadn't bothered to change."

"So we're just listening to music. And I mentioned that I had to get out of my boots. My feet were starting to cramp. That's when things got…different."

"What do you mean, different?"

"Vince told me to move to the other end of the sofa. Then he slowly unzipped my boots and pulled them off. My legs were on his lap. He started to massage my feet, chasing away the aches and pains. Then he moved up to my ankles. And the whole time, he just kept talking, keeping his voice very low and soft."

"What did he say?"

Linda shuddered with the memory. "He told me all of the things he was going to do to me, all the ways he wanted to please me. It was like I was hypnotized. He was in total control of me. I couldn't move."

No words found their way out of my mouth.

"I swear he touched on every fantasy, no matter how dark, I have ever considered. And the whole time, he just kept talking softly, massaging my legs. Jamie, by the time he finally undressed me, I was so far over the edge, I didn't think I'd ever make it back."

FLEEING BEAUTY

A discovery of priceless artwork leads Jamie on a collision course with danger.

Jamie Richmond used to live a nice, quiet life. But last fall she witnessed the shooting of a police officer and figured out who did it. Then this winter saw her best friend targeted by a stalker and kidnapped. Yep, Jamie solved that one and came to the rescue. Now it's summertime and the living is supposed to be easy. All she wants to do is write her novels and spend free time with Malone, the guy who has been by her side since all this craziness began. But that's not likely to happen.

Jamie's father was a very successful sculptor who tragically died more than twenty years ago when she was just a child. What she remembers about him is little more than bits and pieces. A storeroom filled with crates of his work is discovered in an old converted factory. This potential fortune in artwork has been waiting all these years.

Jamie recruits Malone and a few close friends to help her unpack the crates and bring her father's gifts out to the light of day. News of this discovery leads to a robbery. Now Jamie is determined to figure out who is behind the crime.

EXCERPT

This sculpture was titled "Fleeing Beauty".

It was a woman caught in the act of running. Tendrils of slender marble in various lengths and thicknesses extended from her head, as if they were locks of hair billowing out behind her. Part of her face was obscured, turned against her shoulder as if attempting to hide her features from whoever was chasing her. The woman's body was voluptuous, full of dangerous curves. There was something haunting about this piece. The guys became quiet, which was unusual. Linda slowly moved around it, taking pictures.

"Holy shit," Ian muttered.

"Watch your language," Malone said, cuffing him lightly on the back on the head.

"How did he do that?" Ian said, taking a step away. "She looks real."

"She looks alive," Malone said.

"Check the file," I suggested.

None of us could take our eyes off the sculpture.

We spread the file out on the worktable. There were pictures of a woman standing in front of a drop cloth. She was blonde, with an impish smile on her face. She could have been in her early to middle twenties. It was impossible to tell how tall she was. Her figure was eye catching, with a tiny waist and round hips. Most of the pictures showed her in a one piece bathing suit. There was one where she wore a sheer negligee. There were shots of her standing on a pedestal, others with her arms outstretched, and still others where she was looking over her shoulder. In a couple of photos he must have used a fan to blow her hair back.

"She's a doll," Ian said.

"Jamie, I think this is the most beautiful thing I've ever seen," Linda said softly.

"You'll get no argument from me."

STEALING HAVEN

After months of hard work, Jamie and her best friend, Linda, are on vacation. Lounging on the sandy beaches of South Haven, on the shore of Lake Michigan, the ladies *only* plan is *no* plan. No deadlines for Jamie, the investigative reporter. No papers to grade for Linda, the high school teacher. It's time to kick back and relax.

That lasted until lunchtime on Monday, when they shared a table with Jared, a local cop and Randy, a city official who only had eyes for Jamie. Casual conversation revealed a home invasion, which got Jamie's curiosity going.

While the two friends explore South Haven, Jamie discovered a pattern with the home invasions. Sharing her clues with Jared, it isn't long before Jamie and Linda are recruited to help catch the crooks.

Sand, sun, romance and a mystery to solve. Sounds like a perfect vacation for Jamie.

EXCERPT:

That earned me another kiss. This one lasted for about

an hour. Well, maybe it was a minute or two. My hand tangled in his hair, keeping him close.

"Glad I'm different from most guys," he said quietly as we separated. His hands returning to the wheel.

Part of me was still locked on his kiss. Was this really happening? I looked back at Linda. She flashed a wide grin and made a show of slowly clapping her hands together. I wondered if she knew how to drive a boat so I could drag Randy to the cabin below deck. With an effort, I reined in such thoughts.

"So I'm supposed to believe you don't find young women out looking for fun on their vacation and charm them with that smile?"

"You like my smile? I always thought it was kind of lopsided."

I took his face in both hands and turned it toward me. "Maybe a little crooked. But that's part of the appeal." Now I initiated a kiss. His hands slid through my hair, then softly ran his fingers down my neck. Shivers of excitement coursed through me. A horn sounded nearby. He broke the kiss and turned to check the water. Another boat passed in the opposite direction. A man and woman were at the helm, mirroring our positions, caught in the moment and sensuality of being on the water. I bit down on my bottom lip in frustration. I longed for more than kisses but safety came first.

"We don't want to run into some sailboat out here," Randy said with a grin.

I scooted back onto the bench. Maybe a little distance was in order? It might help my racing hormones. "How fast are we going?"

"About thirty. Want to go faster?"

Was he talking about the boat, or the two of us? Randy shifted. His right hand had dropped to the controls, his left lightly holding the steering wheel. He watched me, his lopsided grin worked its magic.

CHASING FAVORS

Doing a favor for an old friend. What could possibly go wrong??

It was supposed to be one simple favor. Randy was the nice, charming guy who drew Jamie into a steamy romance, two years ago, during her vacation. Now he's in town, nudging her curiosity with the request for some help. What could possibly go wrong?

Jamie's skills as an investigative reporter made for a smooth transition to writing mysteries. And Randy's request seemed harmless enough. Doing a favor for a friend is really no big deal. But things are rarely as they appear when Jamie starts digging. When she uncovers the answers for Randy, she's faced with another request for a favor. Who knew she could be so popular? Now Jamie's spending her time, chasing after favors.

While researching Randy's situation, Jamie stumbles upon something that doesn't seem quite right. Most people would just ignore it. Or chalk it up to a coincidence. But Jamie's never been a believer in those. Sensing there is something more going on in the background, Jamie becomes determined to figure it out. And if she's right, she intends on stopping the bad guys in their tracks.

CHASING FAVORS features the beautiful redhead whose nose for trouble has her stumbling into police business. Mark Love's series is perfect for fans of the Temperance Brennan series by Kathy Reichs or Diane Capri's Michael Flint series, where solving a mystery and danger abound. Even though you can read Chasing Favors as a standalone, why would you? Especially when following Jamie through her romance and adventures will entertain you through the night.

EXCERPT:

"Malone, are you telling me that my efforts to elevate your heart rate aren't sufficient to ensuring your good health?"

He chuckled and shook his head. "You know how to get my heart racing. But there are other aspects required for a full-body workout."

"Maybe you need to rethink your routine," I teased from the doorway.

He was sitting on the side of the bed about to reach for his tennis shoes. Now Malone flashed me a wicked smile. Before I could move, he lifted me off my feet.

"Malone!"

"Hold still. I'm going to do a set of curls with you horizontally across my arms." He shifted his grip. One arm was beneath my knees. The other was under my shoulder blades.

"Don't drop me!" I started to reach for his neck.

"Keep your arms at your sides, Jay." He turned around now so that he was holding me over the bed.

Slowly he did a curl, rolling me in his arms as if his hands were reaching for his shoulders. On the third curl, Malone dipped his head and kissed my stomach through my shirt. Then he released me, dropping me onto the mattress from shoulder height. I bounced, laughing in delight.

"We've just created a new exercise." He fell on the bed beside me.

"What are you going to call it?"

He gave it some thought. "Curling the vixen."

"I'm a vixen?"

Malone nodded.

"Hope that's one you're only going to do at home."

"Only with you, Jamie." He gave me a kiss that got my heart racing, then slid off the bed. "I gotta run."

"Sure, leave me all hot and bothered," I muttered.

Malone grabbed his shoes and went out the door. "To be continued."

"It damn well better be."

ABOUT THE AUTHOR

Mark Love lived for many years in the metropolitan Detroit area, where crime and corruption are always prevalent. A former freelance reporter, Love honed his writing skills covering features and hard news. He is the author of the Jamie Richmond romance mysteries, **Devious, Vanishing Act, Fleeing Beauty**, and **Chasing Favors**, along with the novella **Stealing Haven**. His short story, **Don't Mess with the Gods**, was written with Elle Nina Castle and included in the *Magic & Mischief* anthology. Love also writes the Jefferson Chene mystery series, **WHY 319?, Your Turn to Die** and **The Wayward Path**. Love resides in west Michigan with his wife, Kim. He enjoys a wide variety of music, books, travel, cooking and exploring the great outdoors.

You can find him on the links below.

http://www.amazon.com/-/e/B009P7HVZQ
https://motownmysteries.blogspot.com/
https://www.facebook.com/MarkLoveAuthor
https://twitter.com/motownmysteries
https://www.instagram.com/motownmysteries

OUR SYDNEY ADVENTURE
By Tammy Mannersly

I am blessed to have one of those dads who is not just a parent but also a best friend. We share the same silly sense of humor, are both extremely stubborn but also unconditionally loyal to those we love, and we both enjoy the same past-times—country drives, walks along the beach, spending time with the dog, and even shopping! He and my mum are the driving support behind my writing and all my achievements, and I would not be the person I am now without their love and guidance.

One of my dad's favorite times to reminisce about is our *Daddy/Daughter* long weekend to Sydney in 2013. He had arranged the holiday to celebrate my 25th birthday and while my mum didn't love missing out herself, she was supportive of our adventure as the two of them had shared a very similar holiday together only a year or so before. It was because of this that my dad chose Sydney as our destination. He hoped to show me all the sights he and my mum had seen during their own time away. He knew that, though I had been there once before when I was 10 for a quick stop over during a family road trip with my aunt, uncle, and cousins, I was not really sold on Sydney as a city. He intended to change my mind.

The trip was met with a terrible start as I fell sick with a bad cold before we even hopped on the plane. Needless to say, my congested state made the plane journey from Brisbane a painful one, but even that couldn't shake my excitement. I might not have been keen on Sydney as a holiday destination initially, but a holiday—any holiday—especially with my dad was a thrilling concept and we had so much planned! We were going to Darling Harbour, to visit the Harbour Bridge, down to The Rocks, to the Opera House, and over to Paddy's Markets in Haymarket. Dad and I love strolling through markets of any kind, hunting for knick-knacks, beautifully handmade items, and local produce.

We arrived at The Menzies in Carrington St and dropped off our luggage. While checking in my dad mentioned my milestone as the reason for our getaway and the lovely staff wished me a Happy Birthday. After walking the main streets, visiting camera stores for my dad, bookstores for me, we stopped to have a snack at a café beside the Hyde Park Barracks. We sat on the veranda overlooking Macquarie Street, enjoying loose leaf tea and one of the best cheese platters we have ever had. That night we had dinner—oysters, pasta, and red wine—at The Rocks with a view of the Sydney Harbour Bridge brightly lit like a sparkling crown against the night sky. Already my opinion of Sydney had improved, but still there was so much more planned ahead.

The next day—my birthday—we followed the tourists to Circular Quay, snapping daylight photos of the Harbour Bridge, the Opera House, the famous Sydney Ferries, before taking the beloved monorail to Paddy's Markets for even more shopping. When our feet were aching from all the walking, our backs sore from hauling our many purchases this way and that, we caught the monorail back to Darling Harbour and ate dinner in a restaurant high enough to admire the nightlife below. We were exhausted, but happy with full-tummies and armfuls of goodies as we entered our room for the night. But we were met with a surprise upon entry—a bottle of champagne and a sweet hand-written card for my birthday from the lovely staff at The Menzies. After a glass or two and much laughter, we each jumped on our enormous queen-sized beds, one at each end of the room, and star-fished until our tired-limbs tingled contentedly and our beds were rumpled and warm. To this day we still think back on that moment as one of the best.

Our final morning was all big blue sky and sunshine, and after the busy day before we were keen for a slower start. We brunched at a café in the center of the Royal Botanic Garden, relishing in the quiet, green space as we thought over all our adventures and the many good times we had shared. It was sad to think our trip was almost at an end. When Dad next asked me if my opinion on the city had changed, I burst out with, "When are we coming back?"

Sydney had won me over with its eclectic mix of fascinating history, the classy shopping precincts, the contemporary restaurants, and the extraordinary beauty found both in the incredible architecture and stunning parks and gardens. My dad had been right. I had fallen in love with Sydney as a destination and I looked forward to returning in the future. But it was him—my wonderful dad—who had made our trip together into such a special holiday. That is why the memory stays with us, why we both consider it one of our favorites, because we shared it *together*, and I know we will share yet another amazing *Daddy/Daughter* adventure one day soon. Love you, Dad!

DAD'S FAMOUS POTATO FRITTERS

Ingredients:

3-4 Large Potatoes

1 Medium Onion

2 Eggs

2 Tablespoons of Flour or Breadcrumbs

Salt and Pepper

Olive Oil

Method:

1. Peel and grate potatoes and onion in food processor using shredding disk.
2. Drain excess liquid from mixture making sure to leave potato starch.
3. Add eggs, flour (or breadcrumbs), salt and pepper to the potato and onion, and mix thoroughly with fork or fingers.
4. Rest mixture for five to ten minutes.
5. Heat olive oil in a pan to a med-high temperature (until fritter mixture sizzles in pan).
6. With a large spoon, scoop the mixture into the pan and flatten with spatula, forming a fritter-shape.
7. Repeat until pan is full (cooking multiple fritters at once).
8. Cook both sides until golden brown and crispy.
9. Allow fritters to drain on a paper towel.
10. Serve with your favorite sauce or side.

My dad loves to serve his fritters with a tin of heated Heinz baked beans and buttered sourdough toast.

AWARD WINNING CONTEMPORARY ROMANCES
By Tammy Mannersly

PERSUADING LUCY

You can't hide from destiny....

Callum Hawthorne is one of those lucky guys who seem to have it all. He's a wealthy property tycoon, the CEO of his family's company. He's handsome, intelligent and charming and has a gorgeous new woman on his arm every week. But there's one thing still missing – the love of his life, Lucy Spencer.

Fourteen long years ago, Lucy left for college and cut off all contact with Cal, leaving their mutual friend Madison as his only connection. That was until in his effort to save his deceased father's beloved Gold Coast property, The Calypso, Cal contacts Insight Marketing, the best advertising firm in Melbourne, and discovers his Lucy among the team.

Successful marketing executive, Lucy Spencer had managed to avoid her ex-best friend for nearly half their lives. Fearful of trusting him, loving him and having her heart broken all over again, Lucy tries to keep her distance from him, but discovers that there is a fine line between love and hate, and maybe – just maybe – Cal could be her inescapable destiny.

EXCERPT:

Cal was flabbergasted. What had happened? What had he missed?

Then, distracted by her outburst, he made another mistake and his grip on Lucy's wrist loosened slightly. As if sensing his lapse in control, she used the whole weight of her small frame to jerk herself free of his hold and with a triumphant sigh she began to back away.

"So, you orchestrated this together, did you? What, did you seduce Maddy too? Why can't you just leave me alone?"

Cal's gaze narrowed with concern. "What are you talking about, Luce?"

Worried that she'd run before he had a chance to explain, Cal reached out and took a step toward her. But, Lucy immediately backed farther away, taking two steps for his single stride.

"What did you give her to make her finally tell you where I was?"

Her fiery glare was enough to make his fingers ache to touch her, to soothe her. He hated seeing her in so much distress.

"Nothing." His voice was calm, pacifying. "She didn't tell me."

Lucy frowned and her gaze dropped from his, confusion clearly clouding her expression.

"But I—" She shook her head with irritation and glanced back up at him. "But how did you know that I'd be here?"

Cal smiled as he remembered the moment of pure serendipity, the second he'd seen her gorgeous face on the team's profile page on the Insight Marketing website.

Executive Manager Lucy S., it had read. Cal had tried searching the internet for her before, but to no avail. There had always been too many Lucy Spencers and he'd been convinced that she must have altered her name. Yet, this time he'd found her, so simply found her, as though the universe had finally pointed her out to him.

"Fate," he said confidently.

DRAWN TO HIM

The new doctor in town is attracting some attention, especially of the female persuasion, but art teacher, Erica Townsend is blissfully unaware until she ends up injured and in his office. Too bad she'd vowed to resist love—that traitorous emotion, the destroyer of lives—after numerous failed relationships. Something about Matt, about their electrifying connection has her wondering if he might just be…the one.

Dr. Matthew Garrick is tired of playing wing-man for his best friend. It isn't that he wishes to look for love, rather the opposite. But the eagerness of some of the single women in their small country town unnerves him. That is, until a certain stunning brunette appears in the waiting room of his medical practice. Her touch sparks something deep inside him, jolting his heart into a new rhythm and Matt makes it his mission to win's Erica love. Can he convince her to take a risk on him and what they share together?

As the good doctor strives to show Erica that love doesn't have to come at a price, his dangerous secret admirer threatens to prove otherwise.

Whoever said love wasn't dangerous?

EXCERPT:

Matt carefully lifted the white lid of the stylish box. After shifting a mass of silver tissue paper, he noted the smooth, gray fabric of a familiar piece of clothing and drew the item free. It was the same shirt he'd worn to the life drawing class last Friday, the same shirt he'd been wearing when he'd returned to Unique Art Boutique later that night, and the same shirt he'd ruined when he'd torn it off himself to get naked with Erica for the very first time.

Nate touched a smooth gray sleeve. "It's a dress shirt."

Desperate to elucidate the item's importance, Matt opened his mouth to answer but spluttered as he tried to swallow and breathe in all at once. Matt dropped the garment into the box and stepped backward, his whole-body convulsing as he coughed.

"You all right, buddy?" Nate slapped Matt on the back in an effort to clear his airways.

Matt nodded and finally stopped coughing. Straightening, he breathed deeply.

"Thank God." Nate chuckled. "For a split-second there, I was thinking anthrax."

"I think it might be worse." Matt's voice was hoarse.

"It's just a shirt, buddy. How could it be worse?"

Matt's heart raced, his skin becoming cool and clammy. He took another calming breath before glancing down at the elaborately decorated crimson and pink card on the desk. "I own the exact same shirt. It got damaged last Friday night, the first night Erica and I got together."

A smile pulled at his friend's lips, but Matt shook his head.

"No, Erica didn't send this. I think someone else was there that night, watching us."

CAUGHT BY HIM

Dylan O'Day has been an exemplary marine biologist for years, constantly devoted to the protection and preservation of the natural world. Yet lately, he has a new passion, one that's distracting his once focused thoughts. Though a decade older than her and her trusted mentor, Dylan hasn't been able to stop thinking about the new intern. He's never met a person quite like Kyra before, someone so genuine and caring, and who understands his love of environmental conservation. It's just too bad his age and situation put him in an ethical dilemma. Should he risk it all for a chance at happiness or insist on keeping their relationship platonic?

Kyra Shine began interning only a few months ago at the Merchant Marine Science Centre and she's already crushing hard on the boss' son. Jake Merchant might be the bad boy of the team, but he seems perfect. They share a love of nature, especially the ocean and spend their days watching over the endangered turtles nesting along the coast. While her mentor—the sweet, but overprotective Dylan—disagrees with her growing infatuation, Kyra's sure his scathing assessment of Jake is misinformed. Surely, the two men are more alike than they realize.

After discovering the turtle nests raided in the night, the Science Centre team goes on high alert, until a dangerous interaction with illegal poachers shatters reputations. Can the team save their beloved turtles before another nest is ransacked? Will Dylan overcome his concerns to tell Kyra how he truly feels before her heart is completely lost to another?

EXCERPT:

"What are you up to, Shine? Playing with the fishes?"

"Something like that," she agreed, fighting back the girlish giggle that wanted to burst from her lips as soon as those gorgeous brown eyes had met hers.

His gaze dropped and roamed over her body for a moment. His head nodded slightly with the movement. Kyra's nipples hardened under his stare, and the heated tingling of desire clawed at her. Warmth blossomed over her skin. She glanced down, checking that her body was still hidden beneath the flimsy material of the red and white frangipani bikini.

"Lucky fishes," he drawled, dragging his gaze back to hers.

She chuckled, suddenly tense. "You've seen me in this bikini before, Jake. It's nothing special."

"Nothing special." He stepped forward, closing the gap between them. "I would never say that."

His fingers reached up, skimming her collarbone before slipping under the thin rope of material that formed the halter around her neck. He slid them along her skin, the hot, rough, dryness of him against the soft, moistness of her. They caressed their way up to her neck and then back down, just above the cup of the bikini's bra. He let his fingers linger there, his chocolate brown eyes gazing deep into her own.

Jake stepped back from her reluctantly. "What are you doing tomorrow night?"

Her dark blonde brows narrowed as she tried to calm her ragged breathing. "Sunday?"

He nodded.

"That's family night," Kyra began again. "I mean, you know we can't miss family night. Your dad always invites everyone from the Turtle Center and the Science Center for a big barbeque. Everyone who wants to come is invited."

He shrugged. "Maybe we don't want to come this time?"

She giggled. "And, what are we going to do instead?"

Jake reached for her free hand, holding it, cool and damp against the warmth of his. "Go out for dinner. Somewhere nice. Together."

FINDING HIS ZEN

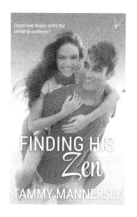

Swimming superstar, Sebastian DuMont, agrees to headline the reopening of the Poseidon's Shore Health Club at a discounted fee, grateful for an excuse to visit his beloved hometown. However, he hadn't expected to be tempted by the lovely Zenia, owner and operator of the fitness facility.

All of Zenia Andino's dreams come true with swimming superstar, Sebastian DuMont, attending her gymnasium's reopening. She'd idolized him as a teenager with his poster pinned to her bedroom wall, but meeting the hunky celebrity in person gives her heartbeat an excited new rhythm.

Before they can test the waters, Seb's agent interferes and Zen's fame-hungry sister alludes to an affair with the Olympian. Will Seb keep up the lie for continued fame and fortune? Or is it finally time to follow his heart and feed the special spark he felt with Zen before the opportunity extinguishes forever?

EXCERPT:

"So, do you think there might be love in the air?" Sara, the reporter from the Courier Mail enquired again.

A wide, ecstatic grin was like a gash across Lexy's face. She gazed up into his eyes, searched them for a second before once again acknowledging the assembly. "When it comes to Seb and me, anything is possible."

At that, the bottom fell out of Seb's stomach and he felt as like he was riding the steep, rushing decent of a rollercoaster dip.

The audience erupted at Lexy's answer, newly galvanized and interested in the possibility of a sexy affair to report on and obsess over. The insinuation of a relationship made Seb feel sick, nausea roiling in his gut. He wanted to correct the mistake, but couldn't see a way out without embarrassing both of them.

Seb felt a pat on his shoulder as the raucous roar of the gathering continued, the audience's arms waving, camera's flashing and he heard Mayor Jones commend him.

"Congratulations," the older man said, his tone genuinely joyous, oblivious to the reality.

With his heart racing, palms sweating, his gut churning on the verge of sickness, Seb cast a look at the one person in the world whose opinion really mattered to him in that instant. He caught Zenia's eye, saw her solemn smile and…seeing that look, her fallen spirt, had pain stabbing into his heart, breaking it a little.

What the hell had he done? What the hell had he agreed to? And what could he do to show Zenia that his true interest lay with her and not her sister?

THE RIGHT BROTHER

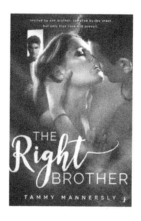

Invited by one brother, tempted by the other…

Former Australian playboy Blake Davenport knows his billionaire brother, David, is capable of anything to ensure he gets what he wants. But manipulating his young daughter's beautiful teacher into marriage is unacceptable.

Gwen Deveraux is grateful for the invitation to spend Christmas and New Year's with her beloved student's family, especially when her handsome host is so eager for her company. After surviving a broken heart, she is finally ready to give love another chance.

But, who with?

The illustrious David Davenport whose real motives

seem hidden behind charm? Or his roguish brother, Blake, who has tempted her heart and body from the very moment they met?

EXCERPT:

"I am waiting for an answer, Miss Deveraux."

Her hands slipped from his face, but he grabbed them before they fell.

"Lost for words, are we?"

Under his challenging stare, all her prior bravado had left her. She nodded. "I can't believe you're serious?"

"And why not? Why should I not take the opportunity to fight for you when you are so quick and willing to offer yourself to my morally bankrupt brother? What kind of gentleman would I be just to sit back and watch you sacrifice yourself to the wicked wolf? No, Gwen, I won't accept your friend request. I choose to throw my hat in the ring. I am not one to back away from a challenge, especially not one I know I can win."

With that, Blake dragged her into his strong arms, trapping her against the hard, bare muscles of his chest. His lips covered hers in a possessive and passionate kiss. Instinctively, Gwen melted into his arms, but soon, sense returned. She broke their embrace and pushed free of him. His smirk in return was both triumphant and charming.

Gwen panted heavily, breathless with a heady mixture of lust and fury. She glared at him, assessing him from a safe distance. "You, sir," she told him as she fought to catch her breath, "are the wolf. And it's you I'll have to learn to keep my distance from."

Blake's laughter in response only incited her anger.

"I'd like to see you try," he told her.

ABOUT THE AUTHOR

Tammy Mannersly is an Australian author based in Brisbane, Queensland. She loves writing romance, has a fondness for animals, is crazy about movies and enjoys a great Happily Ever After. Her passion for writing started from a very young age and led her to complete a Bachelor Degree in Creative Industries majoring in Creative Writing at Queensland University of Technology. Her novel, *Persuading Lucy*, was a 1st Place WINNER in the 2018 Chatelaine Books Awards for Romantic Fiction, a Chanticleer International Book Awards competition.

You can find out more information about Tammy and her work on her website: www.tammymannersly.com or by visiting:

Facebook:
https://www.facebook.com/tammymannersly

Goodreads:
https://www.goodreads.com/author/show/16935790.Tammy_Mannersly

Instagram:

https://www.instagram.com/tammymannersly/
Twitter: https://twitter.com/TammyMannersly

THE FATHER I WANTED
By Jennifer Raines

My memories of my father are few, and mostly of him leaving, or failing to keep his promises. I was lucky enough to have an incredible surrogate father in my uncle, the husband of Mum's older sister. Giovanni Batista—an Italian immigrant, known in Australia as John. Back in the day we tended to Anglicize names. He didn't mind. At his funeral my brother offered the comment "he was always there". And that summed Uncle John up. He was prepared to feed, house, and more importantly, to tease us during difficult times. His love was one of the most precious gifts in my childhood and adolescence, and I never questioned it. His love for my aunt was strong, and he was unafraid to show it. In many ways, he taught me about the kind of man I'd like to share my life with—loving, generous, tolerant, open to new ideas, and absolutely loyal. He was also a looker.

He taught my aunt to cook Italian food, so in a country that drew its cooking styles from bland, repetitive English food, I was introduced to Italian food early. His favourites were simple pastas and salads, with Braciole—meat rolls cooked in a sauce. The local butcher found Uncle John challenging. Veal was not a common cut of meat in Australia in suburban Sydney in the 1970s, whereas crumbed veal was a mainstay of Italian cooking.

Uncle John claimed to be a great cook, so one day the family challenged him to prepare a meal. Artichokes in about eight different ways was his answer. He silenced us all with that meal. The first and only time I remember him cooking. Sadly, the stuffed artichoke hearts recipe, my favourite, is lost in the mists of time.

So I offer you Braciole, regularly served, probably because in the day it was a low-cost meal, and you could introduce variations depending on your mood and the available ingredients. It could always be stretched to include an unexpected guest. My recipe is based on memory, so a bit of trial and error might be needed for it to suit you and your family, but experimentation is half the fun.

BRACIOLE

Braciole is common in Italy, although the recipes vary by region. My version comes from the south where thin cuts of beef (or pork) are pounded until they're very thin, sprinkled with grated fresh parmesan cheese, some crushed garlic, salt and pepper and finely chopped parsley, rolled, then tied with string—that was a ritual. Then you stew the meat rolls in a tomato sauce. You use most of the sauce for your pasta (primo), then serve the braciole with a serving of salad as your secondi.

Ingredients: Meat rolls

Quantity based on the number of rolls per person. Usually one roll per person because the sauce served with pasta has taken the edge off your appetite.

- Meat of your choice (veal, pork or round beef steak) cut thinly, then pounded to be as thin and tender as possible (cheaper cuts of meat work because of the pounding and slow cooking time)
- Grated cheese (parmesan, or other combinations eg. mozzarella/reggiano)
- Garlic, crushed or grated
- Parsley, finely chopped

Ingredients: Tomato sauce

Quantity almost doesn't matter because the sauce is used for the primo course—pasta— and any remaining sauce can re-used. This quantity is for approximately 6-8 rolls

- 2 tablespoons olive oil
- 2 cloves garlic crushed, more if you're a fan
- 1 large brown onion finely chopped
- 400 gms crushed tomatoes (cans are fine)

- 200 gms tomato passata (pre-prepared is fine)
- 1 tablespoon tomato paste (optional)

Method:
- Prepare the meat rolls as above (set aside)
- Using a heavy based pan that will allow the meat rolls to fit in one layer, heat olive oil, add onion, sweat down for a few minutes until translucent, add the garlic, fry for a few seconds. Add the crushed tomatoes and passata and cook for 10 mins.
- Add the meat rolls, cook on simmer for 45 mins or until cooked.
- About 15 mins before the meat is cooked, cook pasta of your choice—penne works. Spoon the sauce onto the pasta and serve with fresh parmesan
- As a second course, serve the meatballs with a green salad.

AUSTRALIAN AWARD WINNING ROMANCES
By Jennifer Raines

TAYLOR'S LAW

Tell me a secret and I'll tell you a lie.

Ella Anderson adores her niece. Despite struggling to make ends meet, accepting her dying sister's request she raise Tessa as her own is a no brainer. Until she receives a summons from a legal goliath on behalf of a wealthy stranger claiming paternity and, potentially, custody of her child.

Jake Taylor has been ripped off one too many times. Yet the letter from a woman claiming his cousin fathered her child feels real. His aunt and uncle are desperate for a grandchild. When the child's aunt shows up in his office in place of the child's mother, he smells fraud.

Secrets and lies bubble to the surface, threatening Ella and Jake's growing attraction. In a minefield of divided loyalties, can Ella trust Jake to make the right decision about custody of Tessa?

Jennifer's book is great for fans of contemporary romances where attraction blossoms into breath-stealing passion, where mutual respect leads lovers to also being friends, and where humour and tolerance enliven a deep and abiding love.

Jennifer likes to think her readers get occasional hints of the deep passion of a Nora Roberts or the unshakeable loyalty of a Grace Burrowes where love conquers loneliness, distrust and fear.

EXCERPT

"Who are you?" he demanded.

The tension in his liquid chocolate voice rippled through her. This man couldn't be Tessa's father. The ferocity of her denial rattled her. Every cell refused to accept he'd been her sister's lover. And some remnant of reasoned thought nagged at her. He'd have eaten Chrissy alive.

"Eleanor Anderson." With an effort, she gathered her professional poise. "Chrissy's sister. Ella. You must be Drew." She reached out a hand.

"You know damn well I'm not Drew."

"If you aren't Drew, who are you?" Off-balanced by his instant attack, she tried to steady her jumpy nerves. Withdrawing her hand, she turned to the older man, who was staring at Tessa. "Mr. Taylor, your letter requested Chrissy meet you here about Drew Browning's paternity and …" She stumbled to a halt over the word "custody," then shook her head as a bizarre idea formed. "You can't be Drew?"

"I'm his father, Peter." His presence confused her further but confirmed the identity of the pirate king.

She stretched out a hand for a second time. "Then you must be Mr. Taylor. Good morning."

"Where's Chrissy?" Taylor demanded.

Before she could answer, Tessa's soft voice ricocheted around the room. "Mama's in heaven."

GRACE UNDER FIRE

It's deal or no deal when a new threat forces two independent neighbours to face a past tragedy.

Artisan cheese-maker GRACE ANDERSON lost her closest friend to suicide, then saw her father swindled out of prime dairy land. Abandonment and mistrust cemented her determination to become the fifth generation on the family farm and to do it alone. A deterioration in her mother's health starts the clock. Grace has three months to buy her parents out—a decade sooner than planned—or lose the farm.

Neighbour RYAN WILSON is haunted by the belief he failed to prevent his younger brother Danny's suicide. He's returned to sell his mother's farm. In eight years away, he's built a fortune flipping farm properties and doesn't do attachment—to land or people.

The bank plays hard ball, forcing Grace to consider Ryan's offer to buy part of her land. The sizzling attraction simmering between them is an unwelcome complication. She doesn't want a business partner, he doesn't want to care, but when someone tries to sabotage her purchase, she finds herself turning to Ryan for more than financial help.

Can Ryan convince her accepting help is not failure? Can Grace escape her legacy of mistrust and teach him how to care again?

GRACE UNDER FIRE is an award-winning story which brings readers along an emotional journey with the complex characters. Jennifer likes to think her readers get occasional hints of the deep passion of a Nora Roberts or the unshakeable loyalty of a Grace Burrowes where love conquers loneliness, distrust and fear.

EXCERPT

Grace had looked to Ryan in the church ten years ago. For help to make sense of the madness? For reassurance? To see if he shared her sense of loss, of waste, of guilt in not being able to prevent Danny's death. Ryan had refused to talk to her after Danny's funeral, abandoning her to suffocating grief.

Ryan had been seventeen then to her fifteen, as tall as now but gangly. He hadn't grown into his build, but the promise of the man had been there. His shaggy hair had been longer. Not long enough to hide his tight, shuttered expression.

The pain of Ryan's rejection had smouldered inside her, only to flare up now. He'd left town straight after her best friend Danny's funeral. Hadn't stayed for the wake or to listen to community condolences. Ryan had spoken to no one. Not even her. Then disappeared. *When his mother needed him.* Grace had struggled to forgive him for that too. She'd taught herself not to need him, not to need anyone other than her family.

"I'm sorry I didn't speak to you." He rose abruptly to his feet, his hands held up in front of him.

She rose with him. Her heart hammered, her hands balled and her legs were planted wide in defiance.

PLANTING HOPE

Can digging and weeding, planting, and pruning equal love?

Nursing is HOLLY COOPER's vocation, and her sanctuary, until she witnesses a murderous attack during emergency surgery. Her childhood fear of never belonging resurfaces. Untethered, she's following music festivals down Australia's eastern seaboard, sometimes working as a nurse, sometimes as a volunteer.

Reclusive gardener CHRISTOPHER (Kit) SILVERTON needs a nurse for his half-finished research project: the therapeutic power of gardening. In plain English, can digging and weeding, planting, pruning, hacking, or any one of those activities help kids to heal after domestic violence? A survivor himself, he knows what it's like to live with pain, guilt, and relationships that end in tears.

When Kit's partner, and on-site nurse, is injured, she suggests her granddaughter, Holly Cooper, as a replacement. Holly has the qualifications, but Kit will need convincing that a pink and green haired free spirit has anything to offer the project.

As the garden develops, passion blooms between Holly

and Kit. When security on the site is breached, Kit confronts his worst nightmare. Defending the kids and Holly proves his critics right—violence lives within him. Can Holly overcome her own doubts to prove he's wrong?

Jennifer Raines's books evoke the romance of Nora Roberts' books but set in the sweeping Australian countryside. PLANTING HOPE proves that love can overcome demons and let our true self shine through. Don't miss this story that blooms like a garden of hope.

EXCERPT:

"You know the dog."

Holly recognised the voice of her caller from earlier in the day. Her gaze travelled up long legs and paused at the work-roughened hand holding the large cat basket where Max peered regally through the mesh. Continuing up, she found a broad chest, covered in a navy sweater knitted in an intricate pattern Mona reserved for those she was fond of. Holly's stare landed on a craggy, square-jawed face scowling at her. His frosty grey gaze suggested his mood hadn't improved. *How come Mona didn't mention her ripped, mid-thirties friend?*

"Christopher Silverton." She scrambled to her feet and offered a hand. "I'm guessing you looked after Bella and Max, as well as Mona."

He refused her offer of a hand, instead doing his own slow survey. She failed whatever test he'd set her. "I've driven past the house a few times today," he said. "But you weren't here."

"Just got here," she replied. The guy needed a personality bypass, but he'd done his second good deed for the day.

"It's after nine."

"Is it?" It could be a hair past a freckle for all Holly cared. She held out her hand. "Max."

"I fed them." He handed her the carrier. "I'll take you to the hospital."

Her eyebrows rose at the masterful tone. "That's not necessary."

"The least you can do is go and see your grandmother. Or"—he leaned closer and his nostrils twitched—"maybe you need a bath first."

"Advice noted." She set the carrier on the floor, then closed the door in his face, deliberately locking it. She braced herself—body and mind—for a pushback, expecting his pent-up irritation to explode in loud knocking or shouted instructions. Nursing had taught her a lot of men didn't take no for an answer. Her heart skittered against her chest. A lot of people didn't take no for an answer.

LELA'S CHOICE

Missing in Malta—A Risk Worth Taking?

Lela Vella has been a dutiful daughter and aunt for the past decade. But her plan to wean her father and orphaned niece off their dependence on her is scuttled when her niece and boyfriend flee Sydney for Malta. Lela suspects her autocratic father of provoking the flight. Lela's desperate to reach the teenager before her father's ultimatums blow another generation apart.

Widowed, Australian international child-protection lawyer, Hamish McGregor accepts Giovanni Vella's request to remain in Malta after a conference to search for Vella's missing granddaughter. Hamish's formidable reputation is built on putting the needs of the child first. He doubled down on his work after the revenge murder of his pregnant wife by a client's husband, vowing never to get close enough to another woman for her to be a target.

Lela doesn't expect her father's henchman to beat her to Malta. Hamish doesn't expect the girl's doting aunt to see him as an enemy.

Reluctant partners, they navigate false leads and unexpected attraction. Can Lela balance her family's demands with her love for Hamish? Can Hamish accept living life is all about taking risks?

Award winning author Jennifer Raines' stories combine a love of romance with contemporary conflicts. Her writing is both relevant and heart-warming. Each story is a journey across the world. Jennifer likes to think her readers get occasional hints of the deep passion of a Nora Roberts or the unshakeable loyalty of a Grace Burrowes where love conquers loneliness, distrust and fear.

EXCERPT:

"Carmen Vella?" He closed the last few metres between them.

Her head turned, her body stilled, her expression unreadable. "You work for my father?"

Question or accusation? He held his palms up in a gesture of goodwill. "I work for myself. I was in Malta on other business, but I've agreed to stay a few days longer to assist you and your family search for your niece."

"I haven't asked for your assistance." Her voice was deep and low, the soft cadence at odds with the wariness he read in her stare. He hadn't expected suspicion.

"Your father ..." he started.

"I'm here independently of my father." She placed careful emphasis on each word.

"Carm—I mean, Ms. Vella."

"Only my father calls me Carmen."

"Miranda, we're blocking the exit." There was a time when saying Carmen instantly sparked the response Miranda—at least in his house, where his grandfather had been hooked on old movies. "Let's get out of everyone's way." He raised his voice enough to explain to a casual onlooker why he'd reached for her suitcase.

"Miranda!" She held tightly to her bag. Her scent, a little peppery, was proving a more reliable clue to the woman than the short bio he'd uncovered in his limited research. "Seriously? Carmen *Miranda*? A 1940s Hollywood star. What century are you from?"

"Give me an alternative."

"Who are you?" she demanded. He was close enough to be singed by the sparks flying off her.

"Hamish MacGregor. I'm an Australian lawyer, specialising in the illegal movement of minors across international borders." He extracted his passport from his jacket pocket and passed it to her. "As I said, I'm in Malta on other business and agreed to provide some assistance."

"To Papa?" She scanned his passport, a slight tremble in her hand.

"Aren't you both pursuing the same objective?"

"I'm not sure of his objective."

ABOUT THE AUTHOR

Australian Jennifer Raines writes contemporary romances set mainly, but not exclusively, in Australia – think Malta, Finland, New Zealand or ? A dreamer and an optimist, her stories are a delicious cocktail of mutual respect, passion and loyalty because she still believes in happy-ever-afters.

Jennifer fell in love with romance as a teenager. Starting with historical romance. Everything in the school library and then a personal treasured collection of Georgette Heyer, hard copies, paperbacks and ebooks. Comfort food, she calls them, like vegemite toast, for those times when she feels low. Her library of comfort food has grown over the years but Georgette Heyer was an early star, under the blankets after lights out using a torch.

Jennifer is a member of Romance Writers of Australia. Three times a finalist in the Emerald competition, including in 2017 (*Common Cause*, renamed *Lela's Choice*), 2018 (*Taylor's Law*) and 2022 (*Quinn, by design*). She's a member of Romance Writers of New Zealand (RWNZ), winning the Pacific Hearts competition twice, including in 2019 with *Grace Under Fire*, the sequel to *Taylor's Law*. She's also a member of Romance Writers of America and has been a finalist in chapter competitions in 2019, 2020 and 2021 (*Taylor's Law*). Jennifer won the contemporary romance section in the 2020 Orange Rose Contest for *Planting Hope* and was second overall. Jennifer placed second in the 2023 RWNZ Koru Awards for Best First Book with *Taylor's Law*.

Jennifer values competitions for the constructive, honest, not always comfortable feedback they provide.

Jennifer loves those days when words flow and the joy of writing makes the hard slog worthwhile. She's always made up stories about strangers in the street, in a café or strolling through an airport terminal; finding inspiration in snippets of conversations, news items and the sheer puzzle of human interactions.

Jennifer lives in inner-city Sydney, Australia, with the requisite number of partners (1) and animals (2). Her desk overlooks a park which nourishes her soul when she raises her head from her keyboard. She gets some of her best ideas during long yin yoga poses or walking – anywhere. While Jennifer adores historical romance, she chose to write contemporary because she thought (wrongly) it needed less research while she was holding down a full-time job.

You can find out more about Jennifer and her writing at https://jenniferrainesauthor.com or via https://www.facebook.com/jenniferrainesauthor

Or https://www.instagram.com/romanceauthorjen/

BEACH OPS
By Annie Grace Roberts

"0-500. Rise and Shine," my father announced, flicking on the overhead light.

I fell out of my bed and hurried to get dressed. The typhoon warning from the night before had been downgraded to a Category 2 storm. Beach Ops was a go!

Family excursions with my father were seldom boring. A career Marine Corps officer, he felt it was his duty to instill in his daughters the most important lessons he learned from boot camp: Discipline, Mental Toughness, and Teamwork. Our outings often involved running through obstacle courses, repelling with ropes, and on one memorable occasion, driving a tank. Today, we were pitting ourselves against the forces of nature. Our mission: Breach the storm-ravaged beach near our home, locate and secure a Japanese glass fishing float for my father's collection.

My father became enamored with the luminous green and blue glass spheres during our tour in Hawaii. Made from recycled sake bottles, the glass balls were used during the 1900's by commercial fisherman to keep their nets afloat in the open sea. Manufacturing ended in 1980, but the hollow balls, their glass tumbled smooth and etched by ocean waves, occasionally washed up on our local beach. My father's first serendipitous acquisition of one had turned him into an avid collector. Competition for these fishing floats, however, was fierce.

After every tropical storm, scores of people flocked to our beach in search of the precious glass balls. To increase his odds of success, my father deployed advanced military tactics. His training in the Marine Corps had taught him the value of the element of surprise and the importance of superior numbers. Beach Ops always began at 0-500 hours, ensuring that his troops (my sisters and I) had reconnoitered and secured the beachhead before his adversaries had finished their morning coffee.

Following reveille, my sisters and I dressed and hurried to our family vehicle. We took our seats, wind and rain lashing the windows, and hunkered down in the back while father drove to the beach.

Arriving under the cover of darkness, we prepared

to deploy. My father handed each of us a flashlight. "We'll head south and keep looking until I say halt. If you find one, shout and signal with your flashlight."

We nodded to show that we understood.

Opening the car door, he issued one final order before we hit the beach, "Eyes sharp, girls."

We marched toward the ocean and fanned out across the beach falling into in a classic line formation. Waves crashed against the shore, their white-capped crests gleaming in the dark as the sea foamed and churned. Knowing that my mother would never forgive him if one her daughters was swept out to sea, my father took the seaward flank, safeguarding his troops from rogue waves.

It was difficult to maintain forward momentum against the gale-force winds, but my father kept us in tight formation, calling out if one of us fell behind. Wind-driven sand scoured the skin from our legs and cold needle-like rain pelted us. Our flashlights illuminated broken and battered remnants of plastic beach toys, shredded palm fronds, and mounds of tangled seaweed that had been cast upon the sand by the typhoon. Eyes narrowed against the wind, we searched. If there was a glass ball on this beach, we were going to find it.

At the midpoint of our operational maneuvers, my flashlight caught the gleam of glass wedged among the twisted branches of a pile driftwood. Could it be? Had I found one?

I flicked the switch of my flashlight on and off, signaling the others. "I think I found one," I shouted.

Excitedly, everyone hurried over to look. Buried in sand, the barely discernable glint of green glass shone among the driftwood. My father dug into the sand

and pulled out…a broken cola bottle. It was a terrible disappointment.

The enthusiasm of my father's troops began to flag.

"It's just a stupid bottle."

"I'm cold."

"I'm tired."

"I want to go home."

As every good military commander eventually learns, there are instances when the cost of victory is too high, and retreat becomes the better part of valor. This was one of those moments. "Back to the car, girls! It's time for pancakes!" My father shouted over the raging wind and crashing surf.

Like most armies, our small platoon marched on its stomach. Energized, we retraced our steps and reached the car in double-time. Beach Ops concluded, we returned to home base.

BEACH OPS PANCAKES

Ingredients

- 1/2 cup all-purpose flour, sifted
- 3 eggs
- 1/2 cup milk
- 2 tablespoons melted butter
- 1 tablespoon sugar
- 1/4 teaspoon of salt
- fresh fruit of your choice (or canned pineapple), cut into bite-sized pieces
- whipped cream

Steps

Preheat oven to 450°F.

In a large bowl, lightly beat the eggs with a whisk or fork. Stir in the milk, melted butter, salt and sugar. Add the flour to the egg mixture, a big spoonful at a time as you continue to whisk. Be careful not to over-mix, to keep the pancake light and fluffy.

Lightly grease a 9"-11" oven-safe skillet with cooking spray or butter.

Pour the batter into a heated skillet. Bake 12-18 minutes, until the edges are golden. Remove from oven and place fruit and whipped cream in the center. Starting at one edge of the pancake roll into a log. Cut into slices and serve immediately.

GHOSTLY AND TIMELESS ROMANCES

By Annie Grace Roberts

WHERE LILIES BLOOM

Lily Deene has a new dream guy. There's just one small problem. He's dead.

Seventeen-year-old Lily Deene has no choice but to spend her summer at Brynmoor Manor in England where there are more sheep than people. She isn't thrilled, but after her mother enlists Simon, the housekeeper's son, to give her horseback riding lessons, Lily decides to make the best of a bad situation. It turns out that it's not all tea and crumpets at the manor house. Long buried secrets are stirring. Secrets that are haunting her dreams and Lily quickly finds herself galloping straight into danger.

Excerpt:

As my eyes adjusted, I could see the vague outline of something lying on the ground. I struggled to make out what it was. At first, I thought a tree had fallen or been cut and left in the middle of the pasture. I stared at the shape, trying to figure out why it was there.

Suddenly, I felt my blood drain away in fear. I opened my mouth to scream, but there was no sound. My breath caught in my throat. It wasn't a log at all! It was the body of a man! I stared in horror at the still figure lying on the ground.

I stood unable to move for several seconds. His body lay so still. I was afraid he might be dead. I forced my shaking legs to move forward. As I did so I became aware that I was not alone. I could sense the presence of someone else nearby, hidden in the mist.

"Whose there?" I called out, my voice trembling with fear.

Silence. I stood still and tilted my head, listening. The hair on the back of my neck prickled. I heard a sound and whipped around frantically trying to locate the origin of the noise. A flash of movement caught my eye and I watched as a ghostly apparition disappeared into the mist.

THISTLES AND THORNS

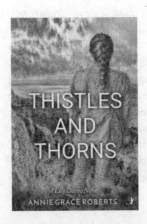

With one ghost on her mind, and another haunting

it, Lily's been ghosted...literally.

Hoping to rekindle her romance with Simon, Lily Deene travels to Anchoret House in the remote Scottish Highlands. Despite a warning to beware of spirits wandering the moors, Lily is drawn to investigate the mysterious death of a young bride, Mairi Morris. She soon realizes that death haunts Anchoret House, and that she too may be in danger.

Lily Deene barely escaped with her life during her last encounter with a ghost, now she's facing another dangerous spirit. If you love mysteries with a little piece of history, you'll love the Lily Deene Series.

Excerpt:

I studied the stonework below Mairi's portrait while he spoke. It was strange, but even I could see that the workmanship was not of the same quality as the rest of the walls in the room. The stones were rougher and not as uniform in shape and color. I reached out to touch one of the stones.

As soon as my hand touched the cold, rough surface, I felt a sudden surge, like the shock from an electrical current charge through my body. It rushed through me, leaving me feeling as raw and exposed as if I had lost a layer of skin. My heart slammed into my chest and the room around me suddenly vanished. I saw nothing but darkness, so black and impenetrable it was like a solid wall. Pain! Sorrow! Rage! Emotions jolted through me, shuddering up my spine and exploding inside my head. I think I grabbed my head with both my hands, but I'm not sure. The only thing I was aware of was the pain as the dark pressed against me, stealing my breath away.

Strangled choked sounds creaked out of my throat. I couldn't talk. I couldn't move. I was like one of the children in Ben's story about the kelpie unable to free myself. Some part of my brain knew I was being dragged down deeper and deeper into the icy black water, but I could do nothing about it. All I knew was pain. Deep, raw pain. I forgot where I was. I forgot who I was. I had no sense of anything except that I was drowning in pain.

UPROOTED

The tangled roots of love and betrayal....

A collision of the past and present. One will find love, the other betrayal.

The last thing Lily Deene remembers is texting her boyfriend, Simon before going to bed. She awakes in the dark and cold with no idea where she is. With air running out, Lily's in danger of becoming a ghost herself.

Nazi prison guard Heinrich Richter decides to leave a war he no longer supports. He undertakes a perilous journey to England and finds something precious he feels he doesn't deserve.

Lily and Heinrich will meet in London where they will find that betrayal and love have deep roots.

EXCERPT:

Something was wrong with me. My head ached and throbbed. My mouth was dry. I tried to lick my lips, but my tongue felt abnormally thick and heavy in my mouth

112

and I couldn't quite manage it.

I opened my eyes cautiously, feeling confused and disoriented. The dark was so complete that for a moment I wasn't sure if I was awake or dreaming? I blinked. I blinked again and I slowly became aware of sensations. Cold. I was very cold.

I struggled to sit up. My arms and legs felt like stone weights. I managed to lift myself a little, but my stomach heaved, and I had to lie down quickly to keep from throwing up.

What was wrong with me? I breathed deeply, drinking in the cold and dark in large gulping breaths as I tried to snag the half-formed thoughts that floated past like drifting clouds. Why was it so dark? Was I sick? Where was my pillow? My comforter? Where was I?

Gingerly, I moved my fingers testing the area around me. I lay on a hard surface, stone or brick. I wasn't in my bed. I should have been in my bed. My head swam with the effort as I tried to figure out what was happening to me. My mind was in a fog. I had no recollection of coming to this place.

Again, I tried to sit up, and this time I managed to raise myself up on my elbows before I felt a sudden saltiness in the back of my throat. Once more, my stomach heaved and roiled. I quickly rolled over and retched, the hot sour smell of vomit permeating the air, worsening my nausea. I lay on my back, too dizzy and disoriented to move. Closing my eyes, I surrendered to the darkness.

ABOUT THE AUTHOR

(photo from 2004)

Annie Grace Roberts is a mother-daughter writing team from California. They share a love of adventure and happy endings. Neither has ever met a ghost they didn't like.

www. AnnieGraceRoberts.com
AnnieGracebooks@gmail.com
AGRoberts_books twitter
AnnieGraceRoberts instagram
facebook: /www.facebook.com/Annie-Grace-Roberts

BECOMING A DAD
By Isobel Reed

In 2023, I became a mother. And I've never known a love like this before. I'm completely, utterly, crazy in love with my little boy. But our journey wasn't an easy one. Pregnancy was rough, and I unfortunately had a few complications. But every step of the way, my husband was, and still is my rock. He happily went out at all hours to buy me chocolate. He reassured me and held me when I cried (which was a lot). And he held my hand at every single hospital appointment - and there were many. Not once did I feel like I was doing this alone, and now that we're parents, it still feels like we are a team. A good one.

Watching Alex become a father has been beautiful. From the very moment our little one was born, he stepped up. He changed the first nappy while I was bed bound after my caesarean. He stayed up when I needed rest. And he made sure I ate even when it was the last thing I wanted to do.

As I write this, we're four months into life beyond birth. Every day, Alex makes sure he spends quality time with our little boy, and it's a joy to watch. Every morning, he takes him on a walk so I can lie in. And every evening, he spends hours playing with him on his mat. It's safe to say that he's a natural when it comes to being a father, and the love in his eyes when he looks at our son shines bright. I can't wait to see what tomorrow brings, and the adventures we will all have together.

The recipe I'm sharing with you today is for the meal that Alex would make me during pregnancy, and after when he thought I needed more protein. It's still a favourite that I ask for a lot!

VEGETARIAN CHICKEN WRAP AND RICE

Ingredients (serves 2):

- 180 grams of tofu/vegetarian chicken pieces (we use Quorn)
- Pinch of sweet paprika
- Pinch of black pepper
- Pinch of dried onions
- Pinch of sea salt
- 1/2 tablespoon of butter
- 2 tablespoons of extra virgin olive oil
- 1/2 cube of vegetable stock
- 30 grams of grated cheddar cheese
- 2 portions of rice
- 2 tortilla wraps

Recipe:

1. Heat two tablespoons of olive oil in a pan.
2. Once heated, add chicken pieces.
3. Shallow fry for 3 minutes while adding salt, pepper, dried onion and sweet paprika. Crush down vegetable stock cube and sprinkle it in the mix.
4. Simmer and stir for 7 minutes.
5. Place chicken pieces into a tortilla wrap, drizzle some olive oil from the pan on top and sprinkle with cheese.
6. Serve with rice on the side.

Top tip!

Once cooked, mix rice with butter and the leftover oil
that's in the pan and fry for 30 seconds before serving.

SASSY AND STEAMY ROMANCES
By Isobel Reed

LOVE TOOLS

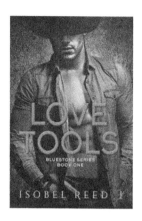

What happens when the king of casual meets the queen of picking the wrong men?

Lily is running. From a dead-end job, a neurotic mother and all the losers she dared to date. Moving halfway across the world to Bluestone County seemed like a good idea at the time. So did reopening her estranged father's hardware store. But now she isn't so sure.

Small town living has its perks though. Wide-open space, clean air, and sexy cowboys. Well, one sexy cowboy. Jake. Who also just so happens to be the new bane of her existence. At least when he's not talking, she can admire the view.

Jake is the king of casual. The love of his life has always been his ranch, and that was fine with him. He never really saw the point in long-term. But all that changes when a mouthy, blonde sasses him into oblivion. He should have known she'd be trouble as soon as he laid eyes on her. Now it's too late. She's all he can think about. All he has to do is convince her that he's finally the right man.

Isobel Reed's hilarious, emotionally charged romance will have you holding your side with laughter or reaching for a tissue. Reminiscent of small-town romance by Tessa Bailey or Kristen Ashley, you will fall in love with LOVE TOOLS and Isobel Reed's unique writing style.

EXCERPT

Lily took the opportunity to scan his face and let her eyes wander down him. His broad shoulders filled out his check shirt that pulled tight across his muscled chest. She tried her hardest not to gawk as her gaze travelled down farther to his mud-stained denim jeans that moulded perfectly to tensed thighs.

Holy shit, he's hot. Do all the men in Montana look like this?

"You about done checking me out, darlin', or do you want me to turn around and show you the back?"

She felt her cheeks flame as her eyes flicked back up and she caught sight of his cocky grin. Before she could attempt to deny what she'd been doing, his expression turned more serious as he gave her a once-over. "I didn't know Matt had a daughter."

Surprise, surprise.

"No shit. He wasn't exactly father of the year."

Lily couldn't help but think of the irony. Her father had become friends with some guy young enough to be his son, yet he still couldn't quite be bothered to pick up the phone and call his own daughter.

Marlboro Man's smile became crooked as his glare intensified. "You always swear like a trucker, darlin'? Here I thought English women were all class and manners."

Is he being fucking serious?

She let out a huff; she couldn't believe the nerve of this guy. "I'm sorry, have I stepped into the past? Are you gonna ask me why a little woman like me isn't married next?"

"All right, sweetheart, calm down." He sniggered, clearly amused by the steam coming out of her ears.

EXPIRY DATING

Sparks start more than a fire... They start an explosion.

Alice is not happy. Her ex screwed her over, literally. One day her mother is dreaming of a white wedding, the next, Alice is hurling hardbacks at a naked boyfriend caught in bed with her best friend. So she did the only logical thing she could think of. She got the hell out of there. In fact, she left the country.

It's not long before she discovers the perks of small-town living, and she even finds herself a job. There is just one thing stopping this all from being perfect though. One infuriating person she just can't seem to shake. Brady Mitchell. It figures that the hottest man she's ever seen also just so happens to be the most annoying one on the planet.

Brady is back home and trying to come to terms with life outside the military. Adjusting to a new job and new limitations from his injury, he expected to settle into a slower pace of life, maybe even a quiet one. That was until

Alice Hart came bulldozing into his world. The woman was anything but quiet. Loud, angry and sexy as hell, yes. But definitely not quiet.

Alice and Brady ignite inside and outside the bedroom. But will they survive the burn?

EXPIRY DATING- the second book in the Bluestone Series is a funny, wild romp along the lines of Stephanie Berget's cowboy romances or Sarina Bowen's True North series. EXPIRY DATING features a retired marine and the feisty young woman who steals his heart. While it is a part of a series, Expiry Dating can be read as a standalone. Grab your copy today.

EXCERPT

There he was—Brady—all six foot two of him. The new bane of her existence. He was wearing a fitted, tan, cop uniform so sexy it should be illegal. If she didn't already know he was the devil, she could easily be fooled by his dark, brooding good looks. Even his damn caramel-coloured eyes were mesmerizing.

Mesmerizing eyes? Get a frigging grip, Alice. He's the devil, remember?

It had been two weeks since they'd met in Vegas at Lily and Jake's impromptu wedding, and despite trying to avoid Brady like the plague since then, he just kept showing up. Yes, Bluestone was small, and Alice was staying at his best friend's ranch, but it was actually getting ridiculous. He was everywhere. Whenever she ventured out, whether it was to get coffee or go shopping, he was there, waiting in the shadows, ready to make her life miserable.

"Looking good, sweetness." Brady smirked as he purposely knocked her on the way over to the fridge, where he swiftly removed a beer bottle.

Alice shot him a glare over her shoulder. "Wish I could say the same to you, Brady, but it appears as if the rumours really are true and beer does go straight to a man's gut."

She was lying, of course. There was no beer belly in

sight. The man was a wall of solid muscle, but something about him drove her absolutely insane. It apparently also meant she couldn't control her mouth whenever he was in the vicinity. He'd somehow managed to crawl under her skin in a matter of minutes of them meeting, and insults had been hurled between them ever since.

Brady's silky laughter bellowed behind her. "You offering to help me work it off, sweetness?"

HERO COMPLEX

Fake it till you make it, that's what they say.

And that's what Ivy was doing. She'd do *anything* to save her ranch. Anything. Including pretending to be engaged to a handsome, retired Marine to placate her sexist clients. Not that draping herself over Ace was a hardship. It wasn't. She just wished he could get over his hero complex and stop trying to save her. There were far better ways they could be spending their time.

Sweet, shy, and babbling Ivy had gotten so far under Ace's skin, he knew he was in trouble. Faking a relationship may have been his idea but he knew deep down he didn't stand a chance with her in real life.

Medically discharged from the military, it wasn't just internal battle scars he'd been left with, he also had some big ugly ones on his face too. If he couldn't even look himself in the mirror, no one else ever would be able to either. Especially not the most beautiful woman he'd ever laid eyes on.

Can these two wounded souls turn their fake relationship into a real one?

HERO COMPLEX- the third book in the Bluestone Series is a sizzling fake engagement story featuring a scarred Marine and the woman who sees only his big heart. HERO COMPLEX features wide open spaces and ranch life along the lines of Becca Turner's Cowboys of Oklahoma series and D'Ann Lindun's sexy Black Mountain books. While it is a part of a series, HERO COMPLEX can be read as a standalone. Don't miss this captivating and heartfelt romance, pick up your copy today!

EXCERPT:

The sun wasn't even up yet, and Ivy was already having an existential crisis. Even the warm, orange glow from the table lamp did nothing to flatter the reflection staring back at her. One thing was for sure though, no matter how long she looked, nothing was going to change anytime soon.

Internally she berated herself. She didn't have time for this. She had chores to do. Horses to feed. And a sexy-as-hell man to try not to humiliate herself in front of.

"Fucking YouTube." She huffed under her breath before dragging herself away from the tilt of her floor-length mirror.

Damn you, Pricilla28! I'm not feeling sexy OR confident. What a load of crap.

There was no time for Ivy to wallow in the YouTube star's betrayal. Or dwell on her poor judgment at trying out a new hair tutorial at stupid o'clock in the morning. Right now, she had things to do. And that meant leaving the confines of her bedroom with her new hairstyle, which was much more male Viking warrior than the sexy, feminine goddess look she was going for.

Damnit all to hell.

Letting out a heavy sigh, Ivy dragged herself and her manly braid downstairs in search of caffeine. Caffeine wouldn't disappoint her at least. Caffeine was consistent. Reliable. Not at all filled with lies.

With coffee brewed, she was just one sip away from bliss when a loud knock had her cursing again. Back was that funny feeling in her stomach. She knew exactly who was at the door. It had been the same person for the past five days now: Ace. Sweet, kind, thoughtful Ace. Quite possibly the most beautiful man she'd ever seen.

Stop swooning and get it together.

LOVE SHOTS

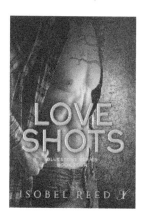

Can these two old friends stop fighting their feelings long enough to grab hold of their second chance?

Summer's life was not going plan. With no job or home, she found herself back in the small town she grew up in. Bluestone County. Despite being broke, she'd always dreamed of taking over her grandfather's bar. So when she found out she was too late and her childhood friend Teddy had bought it, she might have lost it. As in banging down his door and throwing expensive bottles of whiskey at his wall kind of lost it. It wasn't her finest moment. But talking of fine…

Retired Navy SEAL Teddy was used to dealing with tough situations. You name it, he'd seen it. Yet, nothing had quite prepared him for the sight of a raging Summer hurling an eight-hundred-dollar bottle of whiskey at his head. She certainly knew how to make an entrance. And raise his blood pressure. Having the blonde hellion back in town wasn't all bad though. He'd missed his friend. Although he'd be lying if he said friendship was all he was interested in. Summer had owned his heart for a long time. He'd missed his chance once before, there was no way he was going to let that happen again.

Grab hold of this sexy 'friends to lovers' romance as these opposites sizzle through the small town of Bluestone. Alcohol flies, literally, as these two firebrands combust. It's more than the whiskey talking. Isobel Reed's story has all the feels of Tessa Bailey's and Ellie Hall's books combined with the sexy cowboys of Maisey Yates. LOVE SHOTS is the fourth book in the Bluestone County Series but can be read as a standalone, but why would you want to? In this small town, past heroes always stop by for a drink.

TRIGGER WARNING: LOVE SHOTS features a brooding hunk who will do anything to protect the spunky heroine from a dangerous ex who raised a hand to her.

EXCERPT:

"What. The. F**k." Teddy seethed, "I can't believe you just threw a f**king lamp at me!" He could hear his voice getting louder and louder by the second. "What the hell is wrong with you, Summer?"

"*Me?*" Summer's shriek easily matched his volume as her hazel eyes narrowed on him. "What the hell is wrong with *you?*"

A second later, something else was hurtling toward him, only just missing his head. An ear-piercing smash later, he spared a glance at the floor to his left and couldn't help but scowl. This had to be a bad dream. Dark liquid was now seeping into his hardwood floors while crooked shards of glass stood to attention.

"Have you lost your damn mind, woman? That was an eight-hundred-dollar bottle of whiskey!"

"Oh no," she mocked, bringing her chipped red nails up to cup her face. "Sucks when someone takes something that isn't theirs … doesn't it?"

He'd had enough. "For the last goddamn time, Mickey wanted to sell, and I wanted to buy. End of story. You weren't in the country … You're never in the country! How on earth was I supposed to know Mickey promised you the bar? I'm not a damn mind reader, Summer!"

Really, this is all my fault, Teddy thought as he mentally cursed himself. It was too late for this bulls**t. Why on earth did he even answer the door? He was old enough and ugly enough to know that nothing good ever came from answering your door after midnight.

He certainly hadn't been prepared to see Summer Willis. Mickey's granddaughter. It had been five long years since he'd seen the beautiful, blonde, pain in his ass. And now here she was, using the contents of his shelf and his living room wall for target practice because, apparently, Mickey had at one point in time offered her the bar Teddy had just purchased.

ABOUT THE AUTHOR

Isobel was born and raised in London. She still lives along the River Thames with her husband and her substantial book collection. Ever the hopeless romantic, she fell in love with the genre from a young age and was inspired to write her own stories. When she's not feasting on romantic comedies or binge reading her hoard of contemporary romance novels, Isobel is writing.

https://www.facebook.com/isobelreedbooks
https://www.instagram.com/isobelreedbooks/
https://www.isobelreed.net/
https://www.amazon.com/author/isobelreed
https://www.goodreads.com/Isobel_Reed
https://www.bookbub.com/authors/isobel-reed

ABOUT INKSPELL PUBLISHING

Inkspell Publishing began as a dream in 2012 after a number of other publishing houses closed. Slowly, through the years, Inkspell has grown yet still retains a family feeling, as we help authors reach their dreams!

Inkspell has over 100 current releases and many upcoming releases in a variety of genres from Young Adult to Contemporary, from Paranormal Romance to Science Fiction Romance, Holiday stories and weddings. Inkspell Publishing even has free reads, some of which tie into our series books.

You see there's something for everyone. Our goal is to produce quality books that appeal to a wide variety of readers. We are always looking for quality stories and driven authors. You can reach us at http://www.inkspellpublishing.com.